Tales from a Rolltop Desk

Christopher Morley

Tales from a Rolltop Desk

Copyright ...

All rights ...

ISBN-13: 9781647996901

Tales from a Rolltop Desk

The present edition is a reproduction of previous publication of this classic work. Minor typographical errors may have been corrected without note; however, for an authentic reading experience the spelling, punctuation, and capitalization have been retained from the original text.

ISBN: 978-1-64799-690-1

A LETTER OF DEDICATION

TO

FRANK NELSON DOUBLEDAY

Dear Effendi:

I take the liberty of dedicating these little stories to you, with affection and respect. They have all grown, in one mood or another, out of the various life of Grub Street, suggested by adventures with publishers, booksellers, magazine editors, newspaper men, theatrical producers, commuters, and poets major and minor. If they have any appeal at all, it must be as an honest (though perhaps sometimes too jocular) picture of the excitements that gratify the career of young men who embark upon the ocean of ink, and (let us not forget) those much-enduring Titanias who consent to share their vicissitudes. You have been the best of friends and counsellors to many such young men, and I assure you that they look back upon the time spent under your shrewd and humorous magistracy with special loyalty and regard. You will understand that in these irresponsible stories no personal identifications are to be presumed.

I think you remember—I know you do, because you have often charitably chuckled over the incident—that rather too eager young man who came to call on you one day in September, 1913, saying that he simply must have a job. And how you, in your inimitable way, said "Well, what kind of a job would you like best to have around this place?" And he cried "Yours!" And you justly punctured the creature by saying "All right, go to work and get it." (There was more youthful palpitation than intended impertinence in the young man's outcry, so he has assured me.) And then, still tremulous with ambition, this misguided freshman pulled out of his pocket a bulky memorandum on which he had inscribed his pet scheme for the regeneration and stimulus of the publishing business, and laid it before you. How hospitably you considered his programme, and how tenderly you must have smiled, inwardly, at his odd mixture of earnestness and excitement! At any rate, you set him to work that afternoon, with the assurance that he might have your job as soon as he could qualify.

iii

Well, he did not get it; nor will he ever, for he knows (by this time) what a rare complex of instincts and sagacities is needed in the head of a great publishing house; and his own ambition has proved to be a little different. But he can never be enough grateful for the patience and humorous tolerance with which you brooded upon his various antics, condoned his many absurdities, welcomed and encouraged his enthusiasms. In nearly four years in your "shop" he learned (so he insists) more than any college could ever teach: and how much he had to unlearn, too! And the surprising part of it was, it was all such extraordinarily good fun. The greatest moments of all, I suppose, were when this young man was invited by one of your partners (on occasions that seemed so interminably far apart!) to "walk in the garden," that being the cheerful tradition of the Country Life Press. There, after some embarrassing chat about the peonies and the sun dial, the victim meanwhile groaning to know whether it was, this time, hail or farewell, there would come tidings of one of those five-dollar raises that were so hotly desiderated. That paternal function (so this young man and his fellow small fry observed) was rightly a little beneath the dignity of the Effendi: you, they noted, only walked in the garden with paper merchants and people like Booth Tarkington and Ellen Glasgow and good Mr. Grosset of Grosset and Dunlap!

Many young men (O Effendi), from Frank Norris down, have found your house a wonderful training-school for writers and publishers and booksellers. There are great names, of permanent honour in literature, that owe much to your wisdom and patience. But among all those who know you in your trebled capacity as employer, publisher, and friend, there is none who has more reason to be grateful, or who has done less to deserve it, than the young man I have described. And so you will forgive him if he thus publicly and selfishly pleases himself by trying to express his sense of gratitude, and signs himself

Faithfully yours

Christopher Morley

Roslyn, Long Island January, 1921.

ACKNOWLEDGMENT

The original responsibility for some of these stories—or at any rate the original copyright—was allotted as follows: "The Prize Package," Collier's Weekly (1918); "Urn Burial," Every Week (1918); "The Climacteric," The Smart Set (1918); "The Pert Little Hat," The Metropolitan (1919); "The Battle of Manila Envelopes," The Bookman (1920); "The Commutation Chop-house," The New York Evening Post (1920); "The Curious Case of Kenelm Digby," The Bookman (1921); "Gloria and the Garden of Sweden," Munsey's (1921); "Punch and Judy," The Outlook (1921).

All but one of these publications are still in existence. To their editors and owners the author expresses his indebtedness and his congratulation.

CONTENTS

THE PRIZE PACKAGE

LESTER VALIANT came back from Oxford with the degree of B. Litt., some unpaid tailors' bills, and the conviction that the world owed him a living because he had been suffered within the sacred precincts of Balliol College for three years. A Rhodes scholarship is one of the most bounteous gifts the world holds for a young man; but in Lester's case Oxford piled upon Harvard left him with a perilous lot to unlearn. You can tell a lot about a man when you know what he is proud of; and Lester was really proud of having worn a wrist watch and a dinner jacket with blue silk lapels three or four years before they became habitual in the region of Herald Square. But let us be just: he was also proud of his first editions of Conrad and George Moore; for he was much afflicted with literature.

Lester originated in the yonder part of Indiana, but when he returned from Oxford he made up his mind to live in New York. He felt it appropriate that he should be connected in some way with the production of literature, and after hiring a bedroom on the fourth floor of an old house on Madison Avenue, where two friends of his were living, he set out to visit the publishers.

There is a third-rate club in London called the Litterateurs' Club. A few years ago it was in urgent need of funds, and a brilliant idea struck the managing committee. Every writer listed in the American "Who's Who" was circularized and received a very flattering letter saying that, owing to the distinction of his contributions to contemporary letters, the Litterateurs' Club of London would be very much pleased to welcome him as a member, upon a nominal payment of five guineas. About seven hundred guileless persons complied, and transatlantic travel became appreciably denser on account of these men of letters crossing to England to revel in their importance as members of a club of which no one in London has ever heard. And by some fluke the managing committee had got hold of the name of Lester Valiant, then at Oxford—perhaps because he had once published a story in the Cantharides Magazine. Probably they bought a mailing list from some firm in Tottenham Court Road.

Cecil Rhodes's executors paid his five guineas, and he had his cards engraved:

1

LESTER G. P. VALIANT

The Litterateurs' Club, London

The use of these pasteboards brought him ready entrée in the offices of New York publishers. If he had not been so eager to impress the gentlemen he interviewed with his literary connoisseurship, undoubtedly he would have landed a job much sooner. But publishers are justly suspicious of anything that savours of literature, and Lester's innocent allusions to George Moore and Chelsea did much to alarm them. At length, however, Mr. Arundel, the president of the Arundel Company, took pity on the young man and gave him a desk in his editorial department and fifteen dollars a week. Mr. Arundel had once walked through the quadrangle of Balliol, and he was not disposed to be too severe toward Lester's naïve mannerisms.

To his amazement and dismay, Lester found his occupation not even faintly flavoured with literature. He was set to work writing press notes about authors of whom he had never heard at Oxford and whose books he soon discovered to be amateurish or worse. He had been nourishing himself upon the English conception of a publisher's office: a quaint, dingy rookery somewhere in Clifford's Inn, where gentlemen in spats and monocles discuss, over cups of tea and platters of anchovy toast, realism and the latest freak of the Spasmodists.

The Arundel office was a wilderness of light walnut desks and filing cases, throbbing with typewriters, adding machines, and hoarse cries from the shipping room at the rear. Here sat Lester, gloomily writing blurbs for literary editors, and wondering how long it would be before he would earn forty dollars a week. He reckoned that was what one ought to get before incurring matrimony.

***

Like all young men of twenty-three, Lester thought a good deal about marriage, although he had not yet chosen his quarry. The feeling that he could marry almost anybody was delicious to him. But this heavenly eclecticism endures such a short time! For youth abhors generalities and seeks the concrete instance. Also, much reading of George Moore sets the mind brooding on these things. Lester used to stroll in Madison Square at dusk before going back to his room, and his visions were often of a dark-panelled apartment

2

in the Gramercy Park neighbourhood where an open fire would be burning and someone sitting in silk stockings to endear him as he returned from the office.

His arrival caused something of an upheaval in the placid breasts of the two old college friends whose sitting room he shared on Madison Avenue. They were sturdy and steady creatures, more familiar with Edward Earle Purinton and Orison Swett Marden than with Swinburne and Crackanthorpe and Mallarmé. To his secret annoyance, Lester learned that both Jack Hulbert and Harry Hanover were earning more than thirty dollars a week, and he even had an uneasy suspicion that they were saving some of it. When he spoke about Beardsley or Will Rothenstein or the Grafton Galleries they were apt to turn the talk upon Ty Cobb and Tris Speaker. When he showed them his greatest treasure, a plaster life mask of himself that a sculpturing friend in Chelsea had made, they were frankly ribald. Jack was in the circulation department of a popular magazine, and Harry performed some unexplained tasks in the office of a tea importer. Lester was fond of them both, but it seemed to him a bitter travesty that these simple-minded Philistines should possess so much higher earning power than he. So he thought of taking a garret in Greenwich Village, but in the Madison Avenue house he was sharing a big sitting room at little expense. So he spread his books about, hung up his framed letter from Przybyszewski, put his hammered brass tea caddy on the reading table, and made the best of the situation.

Even on fifteen dollars a week a young man may have a very amusing time in New York. For his room and breakfast Lester paid six dollars a week; for his other meals he used to hunt out the little table-d'hôte restaurants of which there are so many in the crosstown streets between the Avenue and Broadway. To come in from the snowy street on a winter evening, sit down to a tureen of Moretti's hot minestrone, open a new packet of ten-cent cigarettes, and prop up a copy of the Oblique Review against the cruet stand, seemed to Lester the prismatic fringe of all that was je ne sais quoi and ne plus ultra. The dandruffians in the little orchestra under the stairs would hammer out some braying operatic strains, and Lester would lean back in a swirl of acrid tobacco smoke and survey his surroundings with great content.

It was while he was conjugating the verb to live in this manner, and sowing (as someone has said) a notable crop of wild table d'hôtes, that he first realized the importance of Pearl Denver. Miss Pearl was

3

Mr. Arundel's personal stenographer, a young woman remarkable in her profession by the fact that she never exposed the details of her camisole to the public gaze; also when the boss dictated she was able to rescue his subordinate clauses from the airy vacancy in which they hung suspended, and hook them up into new sentences capable of grammatical analysis. As a stenog she was distinctly above par, but not above parsing.

Lester, of course, had a speaking acquaintance with Miss Denver, but her existence had never really penetrated the warm aura of egocentric thoughts that enhaloed him. He knew her simply as one of the contingents of the office; and the office had proved a great disappointment to him. Not one of the "firm" (he called them "directors") wore spats; not one of them had shown the faintest interest in his suggestion that they publish a volume of Clara Tice's drawings. Lester must be pardoned for having dismissed Miss Denver, if he had thought of her at all, as not generis.

***

We now proceed more rapidly. Entering the hallway of Moretti's on Thirty-fifth Street, about half past one cocktail of a winter evening, he found the cramped vestibule crowded by several persons taking off their wraps. A copy of the Oblique Review, unmistakable in its garlic-green cover, fell at his feet. Thinking it his own, he picked it up and was about to pocket it when a red tarn o'shan-ter in front of him turned round. He saw the bobbed brown hair and gray eyes of Miss Denver. "Well, Mr. Valiant, what are you doing with my magazine?"

"Oh—why—I beg your pardon! I thought it was mine! I'm awfully sorry!" He was keenly embarrassed, and pulled his own copy out of his overcoat pocket as an evidence of good faith.

She laughed. "I don't wonder you made the mistake," she said. "Probably you thought you were the only person in New York reading the Oblique!"

He felt the alarm that every shy or cautious youth experiences in the presence of beauty, and, with a mumbled apology, fled hastily to a little table in a corner. There, pretending to read some preposterous farrago of free verse, he watched Miss Denver meet another girl who was evidently waiting for her. The two chattered with such abandon, smoked so many cigarettes, and seemed so thoroughly at home that Lester envied them their savoir. Manoeuvring his spaghetti and

4

parmesan, his gaze passed as direct as the cartoonist's dotted line to the charming contour of the stenographer's cheek and neck. His equanimity was quite overset. Never before had he gazed with seeing eye upon the demure creature sorting out Mr. Arundel's mind into paragraphs. Human nature is what it is; let Lester's first thought be confessed: "I wonder if she knows what my salary is?"

At last, after smoking many cigarettes and skimming over the Oblique Review, Lester felt it was his move. He walked down the room, looking at his wrist watch with a slight frown as he passed her table. At the door he saw by the reflection in a mirror that she had not even looked up. He hurried back to Madison Avenue, pausing to sniff the crystal frosty air. At the corner of Fifth he stood for a moment, inhaling the miraculous clearness of the night and pondering on the relative values of free verse and ordered rhythms as modes of self-expression.

In spite of a certain bumptiousness among males, Lester was painfully shy with nubile women, and it was several days before he had opportunity for further speech with Miss Denver. Moretti's is a fifty-cent table d'hôte, and his regimen was calculated on a forty-cent limit for dinner; but after this meeting with the Oblique Review's fairest abonnée he haunted the place for some evenings. Then one day, taking in some copy for a book jacket to be approved by the sales manager, he encountered Miss Denver in the sample room. During working hours she was "strictly business," and he admired the trim white blouse, the satin-smooth neck, and the small, capable hands jotting pothooks in her notebook as she took a long telephone call. She put down the receiver, and smiled pleasantly at him.

"Don't you go to Moretti's any more?" he asked, and then regretted the brusqueness of the question.

"Sometimes," she said. "Usually when I buy the Oblique I go to a Hartford Lunch. I can sit there as long as I want and read, with doughnuts and coffee."

Lester had a curious feeling of oscillation somewhere to the left of his middle waistcoat button. As the little girl said on the Coney Island switchback, he felt as though he had freckles on his stomach.

"Will you come to Moretti's with me some night?" he asked.

"I'd love to," she said. "I must hurry now. Mr. Arundel's waiting for this phone call."

5

A little later in the day, after a good deal of heartburning, Lester called her up from his desk. "How about to-morrow night?" he said, and she accepted.

***

Coursing back to his chamber the next evening, Lester was a little worried about the ceremonial demanded by the occasion. Should he put on white linen and a dinner jacket, becoming the conquering male of the upper classes? But the recollection of the Oblique Review suggested that a touch of négligée would be more appropriate. A clean, soft collar and a bow tie of lavender silk were his concessions to unconvention. He was about to scrub out a minute soup stain on the breast of his coat, but concluded that as a badge of graceful carelessness this might remain. At a tobacconist's he bought a package of cheap Russian cigarettes, such as he imagined a Bolshevik might smoke.

There she came, tripping along the street, with something of the quick, alcaic motion of an Undersmith on high. He waved gayly. She depressed her shift key and reversed the ribbon. He double-spaced, and they entered the restaurant together.

Lester felt an intellectual tremor as they sat down at a corner table. Never had his mind seemed so relentlessly clear, so keen to leap upon the problems of life and tessellate them. It was as though all his past experience had cumulated and led up to this peak of existence. "Now for a close analysis of Female Mind," was his secret thought as he settled in his chair. He felt almost sorry for this gay, defenceless little shred of humanity who had cast herself under his domineering gaze. A masculine awareness of size and power filled him. And yet—she seemed quite unterrified.

As they began on the antipasto he thought to himself: "I must start very gently. Women like men to veil their power." So he said:

"That was funny, my picking up your magazine the other night, wasn't it? You know I thought it was my copy."

"Oh, the dear old Oblique! Isn't it a scream? I read myself to sleep with it every night. We'll have to make the most of it while we can, because Mr. Arundel says it can't pay its paper bill much longer."

This irreverence rather startled Lester, who was writing an article "On the Art of Clara Tice" which he had been hoping the Oblique

6

would buy. In fact, he was startled quite out of the careful conversational paradigm he had planned. He found himself getting a little ahead of his barrage. "Does Mr. Arundel read it?" he asked. "Heavens, no!" cried Miss Denver, and effervesced with laughter. "He would rather face a firing squad than read that kind of stuff. But he has an interest in the concern that supplies their paper." The matter of paper had never occurred to Lester before. Of course he knew a magazine had to have something to print on, but he had never thought of the editors of a radical review being embarrassed by such a paltry consideration.

"Is Mr. Arundel literary?" he asked.

Miss Denver found this very whimsical. "Say, are you kidding me?" she said, with tilted eyebrows. "The chief says literature is the curse of the publishing business. Every time somebody puts over some highbrow stuff on him we lose money on it. The only kind of literature that gets under his ribs is reports from the sales department."

"That's very Philistine, isn't it?"

"Sure it is, but it puts the frogs in the pay envelopes, so what of it?"

"Well, I should expect the head of a big publishing house to be at least interested in some form of literary expression."

"You should worry! That's what we hires for. Besides he has a literary passion, too—Walt Mason. He thinks Walt is the greatest poet in the world."

"Walter Mason?" murmured Lester. "I don't think I know his work."

"Hasn't Walt made Oxford yet?" asked Miss Denver. "He writes the prose poems in the evening papers, syndicate stuff, you know. Printed to look like prose, just the opposite of the free-verse gag." She smiled reminiscently, and quoted:

When I am as dry as a fish up a tree, then I to the hydrant repair, and fill myself up, without ticket or fee, with the water that's eddying there. I drink all I want—half a gallon or more—and then I lie down on my couch; when I rise in the morning my head isn't sore and I don't wear a dark brindle grouch——"

"Is there any free-verse stuff that can cover that?" she asked.

7

Lester was somewhat disconcerted. His assessment of Female Mind did not seem to be proceeding methodically. He played for time.

"I thought you enjoyed the Oblique?"

"As a joke, yes: I laugh myself giddy over it. But I know darn well that kind of junk won't last. By and by the ghost'll quit putting up and the editors will get jobs as ticket choppers. I guess I'm a Philistine!"

With this deliciously impudent creature beaming at him, Lester felt himself cursedly at a disadvantage. Neither Harvard nor Balliol had informed him about this Walter Mason, and though he had seven hundred quips and anecdotes indexed in a scrapbook marked Jocoseria, none of them seemed to bubble up just now. Darn the girl, her mind wouldn't stand still long enough for him to take its temperature. It was like trying to write captions for the movies while the film was running. He blew a cloud of blue Russian vapour across the board, and smiled at her in a tolerant, veni-vidi-Bolsheviki kind of way. Behind his forehead he was fighting desperately to catch up.

As they wrestled with the spaghetti he remembered that someone had told him that publishers usually depend on the literary judgment of their wives. Perhaps that was the case with Mr. Arundel? But Miss Denver laughed aloud at the suggestion.

"Wrong again!" she said. "He's not married. Petunia Veal, the author of 'Sveltschmerz,' has been angling for him for years, and lots of other lady authors, too. He's so sentimental, he's escaped 'em all so far."

She bubbled and chuckled and gurgled her way through the rest of Moretti's menu, amazing him more and more by the spontaneity, sophistication, and charm of her wit. He escorted her home, and then stood under a lamp-post for three minutes removing the soup stain with a handkerchief. "She's immense!" he said to himself. "Why she's—she's a poem by William Butler Yeats!" As an afterthought, he made a mental memorandum to visit the library and look up the work of Walter Mason.

A few days later Mr. Arundel sent for Lester, who hurried to the private office with visions of a raise in salary. The president was sitting at his desk turning over some papers; he motioned Lester to a chair and seemed curiously loath to begin conversation. At last he turned, saying:

8

"Mr. Valiant, your life at Oxford did a great deal to mitigate your literary sensibilities?" Lester hardly knew what to say, and murmured some meaningless syllables.

"I think that your abilities can be of very great service to us," continued Mr. Arundel, "and as an evidence of that I am asking the cashier to raise your salary five dollars a week."

Lester bowed gently; he was not capable of articulate speech.

"I want to ask you a rather delicate question," pursued the president, who seemed as much embarrassed as his visitor. "Do you ever write poetry?"

Lester's voice was amazingly hoarse and choky, but in a spasm of puzzlement and gratification he ejaculated: "Sometimes!"

"What I really mean," said Mr. Arundel, "is this: do you ever write verses of a sentimental nature—hum—what might be called endearments?"

The young man sat speechless in surprise and embarrassment. As a matter of fact, he had been trolling some amatory staves in secret, in honour of Miss Denver; and he imagined they had come in some way under his employer's eye.

"Please do not be alarmed," said Mr. Arundel, seeing his discomfiture. "This is purely a matter of business. As it happens, I have a need for some poems of an intimately sentimental character, and, being totally unfitted to produce them myself, I wondered if you would sell me some? I would be glad to pay market rates for them."

Still Lester could do no more than bow.

"I shall have to be frank," said Mr. Arundel, "and I must beg you to keep this matter absolutely confidential. I have your word of honour in that regard?"

"Absolutely," said Lester, quite vanquished by amazement.

The president's sense of humour seemed to have mastered his diffidence. A quaint smile lurked behind the furrows that years of royalties had carved on his face.

"I want to do some wooing in rhyme; and I want you to turn out

9

some verses for me of a superlatively lyric sort, it being understood that I purchase all rights in these poems, including that of authorship. Would you be willing to do me half a dozen, at say ten dollars each?"

Lester, although staggered by the proposal, was still able to multiply six by ten, and his answer was affirmative and speedy.

"I do not wish to give you any specifications as to the object of your vicarious amour," said the president. "It is a lady, of course; young and fair. How soon can you despoil the English language of half a dozen songs of passion worthy of the best Oxford traditions?"

Jack and Harry found Lester good company that evening. When they got back to the sitting room on Madison Avenue he was lying on a couch, nursing a large calabash and contemplating the ceiling with dreamy brow. As they entered, stripping off their overcoats and chucking the night extras across the room at him, he smiled the rich, tolerant smile of Alexander at the Macedon polo grounds.

"Well, Lester," said Jack, "why the Cheshire-cat grin?"

"I've sold sixty dollars' worth of verse," said Lester, benignly; "also I've had a raise."

"My God!" said Harry. "Think how many starving cubists you could endow on that! There'll be a riot in Greenwich Village."

"Pity the poor bartenders on a night like this!" cried Jack. Then they went to Browne's chop-house for dinner. After a three-finger steak and several beakers of dog's nose, Lester was readily persuaded to enounce the first number of his sonnet sequence, which had accreted or (as its author expressed it) nucleolated, while he was walking home from the office.

"Sonnet, in the Petrarchan mode, item No. 1," he proclaimed:

> Upon a trellis, bending toward the south,
> I set my heart, a yearning rose, to climb;
> It pullulates and blooms in sultry rhyme,
> It spires and speeds aloft, in spite of drouth.
> And seeking for that sweeter rose, your mouth,
> That beckons from some balcony sublime,
> It heeds no whit the tick-tack-tock of Time
> And with its sweetness all the night endow'th.

10

O beauteous rose! O shrub without a thorn!
O velvet petals unsmutched of the mire!
For this my life was manifestly born,
To climb toward thy lips, and never tire!
Now ope thy shutter in the flood of morn—
Lean out, and smile, and pluck thy heart's desire.

"Seems strange," said Harry, "that a man can buy a good meal with a thing like that!"

"What is a petrarch, anyway?" said Jack. "Gee, you'll have to brush your hair to keep it out of your eyebrows," said Harry. "Herod was petrarch of Galilee, don't you remember? It's a kind of comptroller or efficiency expert."

"Nonsense," said Harry. "Herod was patriarch of Galilee, not petrarch."

At this moment Lester was busy multiplying twenty by fifty-two, and adding sixty, and he did not attempt to put Laura's friend right in the eyes of his companions.

***

The next morning, at the office, Lester took occasion to stroll over to the corner where Miss Denver was tickling the keys. Her delicious, able fingers flashed like the boreal aurora; the incomparable smoothness of her neck and throat fascinated him; her clear, blue-washed gray eyes startled him with their merry archness. Wambling inwardly, he met her gaze as coolly as he might.

"Come to Moretti's to-night?" he asked.

"I'm sorry; I've got a date to-night."

He ached in spirit. "To-morrow night?"

She hesitated a moment, tapping the desk with a rosy finger nail. Then her face brightened. "I'd love to."

As he returned to his desk and the dull routine of writing press notes for Petunia Veal's latest novel, he uttered a phrase that he had caught from Harry Hanover. It was the first sign of his emancipation from Mallarmé and the Oxford Movement, for

11

certainly that phrase had never been heard on the quilted lawns of Balliol: "She's a prize package, all right, all right!"

Ten days elapsed. All six sonnets had been delivered and paid for, and Mr. Arundel had bargained for a few extra rondeaux, at five dollars each.

Antipasto, minestrone, breadsticks, force-meat balls, and here we are again at the spaghetti and Hackensack Chianti. Lester had mailed his MS. on "Clara Tice and the Pleinaerists of Greenwich Village" to the Oblique Review that afternoon, and had calculated that the editors could not in any decency offer him less than fifty— or perhaps forty—dollars for it. This, added to 20 by 52 plus 60 plus the rondeaux and other probable increments, would certainly support two in a garret for some time. He also had hopes of selling some obscenarios for the movies. Pearl would probably want to go on with her work, for a while at any rate. She was so independent! But those clear eyes of hers, like a March sky with teasings of April in it, how tender and laughing they were! A few nights ago they had taken a long bus ride together, and she had forgotten her muff. She let him warm her hands instead. He went home that night feeling strong enough to bite lamp-posts in two, and had waked up Jack and Harry to put them right about Petrarch.

Pearl was teaching Lester to twirl up his spaghetti with fork and spoon, instead of draping it out of his mouth like Spanish moss. Suddenly she laughed.

"What did I tell you!" she said. "The dear old Oblique has gone blooie! Mr. Arundel called up the editor to-day and told him the Barmecide Company won't supply him with any more paper until he pays his bills. Of course that means he'll have to quit."

Lester was touched in two vital spots: his own private hopes, and his zeal for fly-specked literature. "Shades of Frank Harris!" he cried. "If that isn't just like Arundel! Why, that man is pure and simple bourgeois! I never heard of such a thing. Has he no feeling at all for art?" Pearl laughed—the pure, musical laugh of careless girlishness, but the recording angel caught in the nimble chords a faint overtone of something else—like the tinkle of ice in a misty tumbler. "Oh, he has his own ideas about art," she said. "He's taken to writing poetry himself. You never heard such stuff—I've been meaning to tell you. What does 'pullulate' mean?"

Lester's valiant heart, Lester's manly hands that had acted as a muff

12

on a Riverside Drive bus, trembled and stiffened. "It 'pullulates and blooms in sultry rhyme," she quoted gayly. "Now what do you make of that, as referring to Mr. Arundel's heart? Sultry is right, too!" Lion-hearted Harvard, oak-bosomed Balliol, and all the mature essences of manhood were needed to keep Lester calm. How had she seen these secret strains? She must have been peeping into the chief's private correspondence. He hesitated during six inches of spaghetti. "Search me!" he said. "Is it in Walter Mason?"

"No, it's his own stuff, I tell you. O beauteous rose! O shrub without a thorn!" she chanted, and her laughter popped like a champagne cork. The horrid truth burst upon him. The boss was courting the angel of the office with the very ammunition that Lester himself had furnished, and his vow of secrecy forbade him to disclose the truth. Oh, the paltry meanness of fate, the villainy of circumstance! It is impossible to describe the pangs it cost him to dissemble, cloak, disguise, and conceal the anguish he felt. But dissemble, cloak, disguise, and conceal he did, and though his heart glowed like an angry cigar stub, he reached home at last.

There he sat down at his table, and amid the healthy snores of his roommates he concocted a fine piece of literary ordnance. Late and grimly he toiled and contrived. At length he had fashioned a sonnet which would be the golden sum and substance of the previous sequence; a cry of the heart so splendidly forensic that Mr. Arundel would pounce upon it, yielding his crisp steel engraving in return. But see, the asp concealed in the basket of fruit, the adder in the woodpile! Read Lester's sonnet as an acrostic:

> *Over that trellis where the moon distills*
> *My heart is climbing like a rambler rose:*
> *You lean and listen to the whippoorwills,*
> *Heedless of how the fragrant blossom grows!*
>
> *O beauteous rose! O shrub without a thorn!*
> *When wilt thou realize my love in sooth?*
> *I touch the windowsill with heart forlorn,*
> *Hoping the guerdon of thy bounteous youth.*
> *After the grief and teen of bitter days,*
> *Troubled by woes that cicatrize and burn,*
> *Ever at eventide I seek thy praise,*
> *Yearning thy maiden bliss—I yearn, I yearn!*
> *Over the rotten fruit of buried years*
> *Unbar the bolt—have pity on my tears!*

The discerning reader will spot the glittering falchion of malice lurking in the initial letters. Read them downward, they convey: o my how I hate you! Lester had but to convey this poisoned comfit to his chief: then, playing upon the artless Pearl, persuade her to show it to him—point out the murderous duplicity of the love token; and she would recoil into his arms. Greenwich Village would sound the timbrel of joy, and even the Oblique might find a softer-hearted papyrus vendor. Vos plaudite! With such thoughts, amid the wailing matin song of boarding-house steam pipes, our hero fell into a brief slumber.

That morning Lester hastened to the office. He waited feverishly until the hour when the chief usually arrived, then visited the private office. There he found the vice-president going over the morning mail. "Is—is Mr. Arundel in?" he stammered.

"Mr. Arundel isn't here to-day," said the vicepresident. "He will be away two weeks."

Lester retired queasily, and hurried to the corner sacred to Miss Denver. Here he found one of the other stenographers using Pearl's machine.

"Where's Miss Denver?" he asked.

The young lady, of humorous turn, looked at her wrist watch. "Getting ready to go over the top," she said.

"What do you mean?"

"Haven't you heard? She marries the boss this morning."

ADVICE TO TO LOVELORN

I

MISS ANN AUSTIN came briskly into her little cupboard of a room at the back of the Evening Planet office. She hung up her hat and coat, opened her rolltop desk, put her small handbag carefully in a drawer, and looked at herself in a greenish mirror that hung secretly on a hook in the recess under the pigeonholes. She took the rubber hood off her typewriter, poured three paper cupfuls of drinking water on the potted geranium on the windowledge, wound up the cheap clock on top of the desk, and moved it forward ten minutes to compensate for what it had lost during the night. Now she was ready for work. As she wound up the clock, the usual thought occurred to her—when would she be able to buy herself the handsome little wrist watch she coveted? There were a lot of them in the jeweller's shop on Park Row, and she admired them every morning on her way to the office. But when one is supporting one's self and an invalid mother in an uptown apartment, and has to pay for a woman to come in during the day to lend a hand, all on fifty dollars a week, in an era of post-bellum prices, wrist watches have to wait. However, as Ann made the daily correction in her laggard clock she used to say to herself: "There's a better time coming." She was not devoid of humour, you see.

Then the office boy would bring in the big pile of morning mail, grinning as he laid it on the pullout slide of her desk. He may be excused for grinning, because Ann was the kind of creature who would bring a smile to the surliest face. She was just a nice size, with a face that was both charming and sensible, and merry brown eyes (when it wasn't too close to the first of the month). Also, that pile of mail was rather amusing. Those letters, so many of them written on cheap pink or blue stationery and addressed in unsophisticated handwriting, were not directed to Miss Ann Austin, but to "Cynthia," and the office boy knew pretty well the kind of messages that were in them. For Ann, under the pseudonym of "Cynthia," conducted the Planet's department of Advice to the Lovelorn, and daily several score of puzzled or distracted beings bared their hearts to her. The pile of letters was growing bigger, too. The Planet, which was not a very flourishing paper just at that time, had started the Advice to the Lovelorn department a few months before, and had put Ann in charge of it because she had done so well writing sob stories. It was beginning to "pull" quite surprisingly as a circulation feature, especially since her smiling little picture, vignetted in a cut with a border of tiny hearts, had been put at the head of the column. Under the cut was the legend: "Cynthia, a Sympathetic Adviser in Matters of the Heart." Ann didn't know whether to be pleased or not at the growing popularity of her feature. This was not quite the kind of thing she had hoped for when she entered the newspaper world. But—the more letters there were from the lovelorn, the sooner she might get that needed raise.

With a little sigh she got out her penknife, began slitting the envelopes, ceased to be Ann Austin and became Cynthia, the sage and gentle arbiter over her troubled parliament of love.

It was a task that required no small discretion and tact, because Cynthia, whatever her private misgivings, tried to perform it with some honest idealism. In the first place, the letters that were obviously merely humorous, or were amorous attempts to inveigle her into private correspondence, were discarded. Then the letters to be used in the next day's column had to be selected, and laid aside to be printed with her comment on the ethical or sociological problems involved. The remaining letters had all to be answered, and data noted down that would be useful in compiling the pamphlet "1001 Problems of Courtship" that the managing editor insisted on her preparing. He said it would be great circulation dope. Ann didn't care much for the managing editor, Mr. Sikes. He had a way of coming into her room, closing the door behind him, leaning over her desk, and saying: "Well, how's little Miss Cupid?" If it hadn't been for that habit of his, Ann would have spoken to him about a raise before now. But she had an uneasy feeling that it would not be pleasing to put herself in the position of asking him favours. She would have been still more disturbed if she had known that some of the boys in the city room used to talk about "Cupid and Sikey" when they saw him visit her room. They said it angrily, because Ann was a general office favourite. Even the coloured elevator man had brought his wooing problems to her one day, wanting to be reassured as to his technique.

It is all very well for you to scoff, superior reader, but letters such as Ann had to read every morning bring an honest pang to an understanding heart; particularly when that heart is in collaboration with twenty-two years of bright, brown-eyed, high-spirited girlhood. Perhaps you don't realize how many of us are

16

young and ignorant and at work in offices, and absorbed, out of working hours, in the universal passion. A good many make shift to be cynical and worldly-wise in public, but who knows how ravishingly sentimental we are in private? Some say that Doctor Freud didn't tell the half of it. As that waggish poet Keith Preston has remarked,

> Love, lay thy phobias to rest,
> Inhibit thy taboo!
> We twain shall share, forever blest,
> A complex built for two!

A complex built for two was the ambition of most of Ann's correspondents; but mainly her letters exhibited the seamy side of Love's purple mantle. You see, when lovers are perfectly happy, they don't write to the papers about it. And when she pondered gravely over "Brokenhearted's" letter saying that she has just learned that a perfectly splendid fellow she is so infatuated with has a wife and three children in Detroit; or over "Puzzled's" inquiry as to whether she is "a bum sport" because she wouldn't let the dark young man kiss her good-night, she sometimes said to herself that Napoleon was right. Napoleon, you remember, remarked that Love causes more unhappiness than anything else in the world. And then she would turn to her typewriter, and put under "Puzzled's" inquiry:

No, "Puzzled," do not let him kiss you unless you are betrothed. If any one is a "bum sport" it is he for wanting to do so. If he "always kisses the girls good-night when he has had a good time," he is not your sort. A man that does not respect a girl before marriage will certainly not respect her afterward.

After she had typed these replies she always hastily took the paper out of her typewriter and tucked it away in her desk. She did not like the idea of Mr. Sikes coming in and reading it over her shoulder, as he had done once. That was the time she had used the quotation "Pains of Love are sweeter far than all other pleasures are" in answering "Desolate." The managing editor had repeated the verse in a way that both angered and alarmed her.

This particular morning, among the other letters was one that interested her both by the straightforward simplicity of its statement and by the clear, vigorous handwriting on sensible plain notepaper. It ran thus:

Dear Cynthia:

I am a young business man, very much in love, and I need your help. I have fallen in love with a girl who does not know me. I do not even know her name but I know her by sight, and I know where she works. She looks like the only one for me, but I don't want to do anything disrespectful. Would it be a mistake for me to call at her office and try to get a chance to meet her? Do you think she would be offended? She looks very adorable. Please tell me honestly what you think.

Respectfully yours,

Sincerity.

Wearied by the maunderings of many idiotic flappers and baby vamps, this appeal attracted her. She put it into the column for the following day, writing underneath it:

You never can tell, "Sincerity"! It all depends upon you. If you are the right kind of man, she ought not to be offended. Why not take a chance? Faint heart never won fair lady.

It was trying enough, Ann used to think, to have to pore over the troubles of her lovelorn clients on paper; but the worst times were when they came to call on her at the office. Fortunately this did not happen very often, for the stricken maidens and young Lochinvars who make up the chief support of such columns as hers are safely and busily shut up among typewriters and filing cases during the daytime; their wounds do not begin to burn intolerably until about five-thirty p.m. But now and then some forlorn and baffled creature would find his or her way to "Cynthia" and ask her advice. She would listen sympathetically, apply such homely febrifuge as her inexperienced but wise heart suggested to her, and after the patient had gone she would add the case to her list of 1001 Problems. The material for the pamphlet was growing rapidly.

One morning, while the managing editor was in her room asking her how soon the booklet would be ready, the office boy brought in a card neatly engraved Mr. Arthur Caldwell. Now as a rule Cynthia did not see masculine visitors, because (after one or two trying experiences) she had found that they were inclined to transfer to her the heart that someone else had bruised. But in this case she welcomed the caller because Mr. Sikes was being annoyingly facetious. He had looked over her laboriously gathered data for the 1001 Problems, and had said: "Well, you're getting to be quite an experienced little girl in these matters, hey?" He had seemed disposed to linger on the topic with pleasure. Therefore Cynthia told the office boy to send Mr. Caldwell in, though the name meant nothing to her. Mr. Sikes went out, and the caller was introduced.

Mr. Caldwell proved to be a young man, quite as nice-looking as the collar-advertising young men without being so desperately handsome. Cynthia liked him from the first glance. There was something that seemed very genuine about his soft collar and his candid, clean-shaven face and the little brown brief-case he carried. He had on brown woollen socks, too, she noticed, in one of those quick feminine observations. He seemed very embarrassed, and his face suddenly went ruby red.

"Is this Cynthia?" he said.

"Yes," said Ann, pushing aside a mass of lovelorn correspondence, and wondering what the trouble could be.

"My name's Caldwell," he said. "Look here, I suppose you'll think me an awful idiot, but I wanted to ask your advice. I—I wrote you a letter the other day, and your answer in the column made me think that perhaps you wouldn't mind giving me some help. I wrote that letter signed 'Sincerity'."

He was obviously ill at ease, and Ann tried to help him out.

"I remember the letter perfectly," she said. "Did you take my advice?"

"Well, I'm a bit uncertain about it," he said.

"I just wanted to explain to you a little more fully, and see what you think. You see I happened to see this girl one day, going into her office. I suppose the idea about love at first sight is all exploded, but I had a hunch as soon as I saw her that——Oh, well, that I would like to know her. I've seen her going in and out of the building, but she has never seen me, never even heard of me. I don't know any one who can introduce me to her, and I can't just walk up to her and tell her I'm crazy about her. They don't do that except in Shakespeare. I don't know much about girls and I thought maybe you could suggest some way in which I could meet her without frightening her."

Ann pondered. She liked the young man's way of putting his problem, and it was plain from his genuine embarrassment that he was sincere.

19

"I'd love to help you, if I could," she said. "It seems to me that the only way to go about it is to arrange some business with the firm she works for, and try to meet her that way. Couldn't that be done?"

"She's secretary to one of the big bugs in the Telephone Company," he said. "I'm in the publishing business. I don't see any way in which I could fake up a business connection there. The worst of it is, there may be a dozen fellows in love with her already, for all I know. I suppose I might get a job with the Telephone Company, but by the time I had worked up far enough to have an excuse for going into the vice-president's office where she works, someone else might have married her." He laughed, a boyish, ingratiating chuckle.

"It does seem pretty hard," said Ann. "I don't know what to say." She had a mental picture of the unknown fair one, going in and out of the big Telephone Company's building on Dey Street, unaware of the admiring glances of this bashful admirer. "I'll bet the men she knows aren't half as nice as he is," she said to herself.

"I happen to know that she reads your column," said Caldwell. "I suppose there isn't any way I could get in touch with her through that?"

"If there's any legitimate way I can help," Ann said, "I'll be glad to. But I hardly see what I can do."

"Well, thanks awfully," he said. "If I get a chance to meet her, will you let me come in again and tell you about it? Perhaps you would let me mention your name as a reference, in regard to my respectability I mean?"

"Surely you can give her better references than that? You see, I don't know so very much about you, Mr. Caldwell."

"In matters like this," he said, "I guess you're the Big Authority. And by the way, do you ever do any book reviewing? I work for Fawcett and Company, the publishers, and we'd like immensely to have your comment on some of our love stories. Can I send you some books?"

"I can't promise to review them," said Ann, rather pleased, because this seemed to her a way to earn a little extra money. "But I'll speak to the literary editor, and we'll see."

"Suppose I send them to your home address," said Caldwell. "I know what a newspaper office is, if I send them here someone else might snitch them. Give me your street number, and you'll be spared the trouble of taking them home to read."

"That's very kind of you," said Ann. "Miss Ann Austin, 527 West 150th Street. Well, you let me know what happens about your fair lady. I wish you all sorts of luck!"

When Arthur Caldwell got outside the office, he looked down Park Row to where the great Telephone Building rose up behind the brown silhouette of St. Paul's.

"Caldwell," he said to himself, "you're an infernal liar! But it pays! I'll figure out some way. While there's life there's dope."

He set out for the subway, but paused again to meditate.

"Ann Austin!" he said. "By George, she's a queen."

II

It is not the purpose of this tale to tell in detail how Arthur Caldwell laid siege to Ann Austin. He was a cautious man, and for some time he contented himself by presenting occasional reports of his progress with the damsel of the Telephone Company. Ann, in her friendly and unselfish way, was delighted to hear, a few days later, that he had met his ideal. Then, averring that he needed further counsel, Arthur persuaded her to have lunch with him one day; and Ann, convinced that the young man was in love with someone else, saw no reason why this should not be done. Perhaps it was a little odd that at their various meetings they should have talked so much of themselves, their ambitions, the books they had been reading, and so on; and so little of the Telephone lady. But surely it was strictly a matter of business that Arthur should send Miss Austin some of Fawcett's novels, for her to review in the Planet; and equally a professional matter that he should discuss with her her opinion of them. And then came the day when Arthur called up to say that things were going so well with the Telephone lady that he wanted Cynthia to meet her; and would she join them in St. Paul's Churchyard at half-past twelve? Ann, with just a curious little unanalyzed twinge in her heart, agreed to do so.

But when she reached the bench in the graveyard, where a bright autumn sunshine filled the clearing among those tremendous buildings, Arthur was there alone.

"Where's Alice?" said Ann, innocently—for such was the name Arthur had always given the lady of the Telephone Company.

"She couldn't come," he said. "But I want to show you her picture."

They sat down on the bench, and he took out of his pocket a copy of the noon edition of the Planet. He turned to the feature page, and displayed the little cut of Cynthia at the head of the Lovelorn column.

"There," he said, stoutly (though his heart was tremulous within him), "there, you adorable little thing, there she is."

It would be pleasant to linger over this scene, but, as I have just said, this is not our denouement, but only an incident. Ann, shot through with delicious pangs of doubt and glory and anger, asked for explanations.

"And do you mean to say there never was any Alice, the beautiful Telephone blonde?" she said. "What a fraud you are!"

"Of course not," he said. "You dear, delightful innocent, I just had to cook up some excuse for coming up to see you. And you can't be angry with me now, Ann, because in your own answer to Sincerity's letter you said the girl ought not to be offended. You told me to take a chance! Just think what self-control I had, that first time I came up to see you, not to blurt out the truth." And then he tore off a scrap of margin from the newspaper and measured her finger for a ring.

III

There were happy evenings that winter, when Ann, after finishing her stint at the office, would hasten up their rendezvous at Piazza's little Italian table d'hote. Here, over the minestrone soup and the spaghetti and that strong Italian coffee that seems to have a greenish light round the edges of the liquid (and an equally greenish taste), they would discuss their plans and platitudes, just as lovers always have and always will. As for Ann, the light of a mystical benevolence shone in her as she conned her daily pile of broken hearts in the morning mail. More than ever she felt that she, who had seen the true flame upon the high altar, had a duty to all perplexed and random followers of the gleam who had gone astray

22

in their search. Aware more keenly that the troubled appeals of "Tearful" and "Little Pal," however absurd, were the pains of genuine heartache, she became more and more tender in her comments, and her correspondence grew apace. Now that she knew that her job need not go on forever she tried honestly to run the column with all her might. How stern she was with the flirt and the vamp and the jilt; how sympathetic with the wounded on Love's great battle-field. "Great stuff, great stuff!" Mr. Sikes would cry, in his coarse way, and complimented her on the increasing "kick" of her department. Knowing that he attributed the accelerated pulse of the Lovelorn column to mere cynicism on her part, she did not dare wear her ring in the office for fear of being joked about it. She used to think sadly that because she had made sympathy with lovers a matter of trade, she herself, now she was in love, could hope for no understanding. Although she hardly admitted it, she longed for the day when she could drop the whole thing.

One evening Arthur met her at Piazza's, radiant. He was going off on a long business trip for his publishing house, and they had promised him a substantial raise when he returned. They sat down to dinner together in the highest spirits. Arthur, in particular, was in a triumphant mood: the publishing world, it seemed, lay under his feet.

"Great news, hey?" he said. "We'll be able to get married in the spring, and you can kick out of that miserable job."

"But, Arthur," she said, "you know I have to take care of Mother. Don't you think it would be wiser if I went on with the work for a while, until your next raise comes? It would help a good deal, and we'd be able to put a little away for a rainy day."

"What?" he said. "Do you think I'm going to have my wife doing that lovelorn stuff in the paper every day? It'd make me a laughing stock if it ever got out. No, sir! I haven't said much about it, because I knew it couldn't be helped; but believe me, honey, that isn't the right kind of job for you. I've often wondered you didn't feel that yourself."

Ann was a little nettled that he should put it that way. Whatever her private distaste for the Lovelorn column, it had served her well in a difficult time, and had paid the doctor's bills at home. And she knew how much honest devotion she had put into the task of trying to give helpful counsel.

"At any rate," she said, "it was through the column that we first met."

What evil divinity sat upon Arthur's tongue that he could not see this was the moment for a word of tenderness? But a young man flushed with his first vision of business success, the feeling that now nothing can prevent him from "making good," is likely to be obtuse to the finer shades of intercourse.

"Of course, dear, I could see you were different from the usual sob sister of the press," he said. "I could see you didn't really fall for that stuff. It's because I love you so, I want to get you out of that cheap, degrading sensational work. Most of those letters you get are only fakes, anyway. I think Love ought to be sacred, not used as mere circulation bait for a newspaper."

Ann was a high-spirited girl, and this blunt criticism touched her in that vivid, quivering region of the mind where no woman stops to reason. But she made an honest attempt to be patient.

"But, Arthur," she said; "there's nothing really cheap and degraded in trying to help others who haven't had the same advantages we have. I know a lot of the letters I print are silly and absurd, but not more so than some of the books you publish."

"Now, listen," he said, loftily, "we won't quarrel about this. I don't want you to go on with the job, that's all. It isn't fair to you. You may take the work seriously, and put all sorts of idealism into it, but it's not the right kind of job for a refined girl. How about the men in the office? I'll bet I know what they think of it. They probably think it's a devil of a good joke, and laugh about it among themselves. Don't you think I've seen that managing editor leering at you? That sort of thing cheapens a girl among decent men. Every Lovelace in town feels he has a right to send you mash-notes, I guess."

Ann was furious.

"Well, you're the only one I ever paid any attention to," she said, blazing at him. "I'm sorry you think I've cheapened myself. I guess I have, by letting you interfere with my affairs."

She slipped the ring from her finger, and thrust it at him. Arthur saw, too late, what he had done. She listened in scornful silence to his miserable attempts to console her, which were doubly handicapped by the old waiter hovering near. She was still adamant while he took her up town. The only thing she said was when she reached the door of her apartment.

"I don't want you to cheapen yourself. You needn't come any more."

By this time Arthur also was thoroughly angry. The next morning he went away on his business trip, realizing for the first time that he who has the pass key to a human heart treads among dangerous explosives.

IV

How different the little room in the Planet office looked to Ann when she returned, with a sick heart, to her work the next morning. Everything was just the same—the geranium on its windowledge, that seemed to survive both the eddying hot air from the steampipes beneath it and the daily douche of iced drinking water; the noisily ticking inaccurate little clock; the dusty typewriter. All were the same, and there was the pile of morning letters from Love's battered henchmen. To office boy and casual reporter Ann herself seemed the usual cheerful charmer with her crisp little white collar and dark, alluring hair. Her swift, capable hands sped over the pile of letters, slitting the envelopes and sorting the outcries into some classification of her own. Outwardly nothing had altered, but everything seemed to have lost its meaning. What a desolate emptiness gaped beneath the firm routine of her daily life. She was struck by the irony of the fact that the only one in the office who seemed to notice that something was amiss was the one person whom she disliked—Mr. Sikes. He came in about something or other, and then stayed, looking at her intently.

"You look sick," he said. "What's the matter, is the love feast getting on your nerves?"

With a queer twitching at the corners of her mouth, she forced herself to say some trifling remark. He leaned over her and put his hand on hers. She caught the strong cigarry whiff of his clothes, which sickened her.

"Too much love in the abstract," he said, insinuatingly. "What you need is a little love in the concrete."

If he—or any one—had spoken tenderly to her, she would have burst into tears. But the boorishness of his words was just the tonic she

25

needed. She looked at him with flashing eyes, and was about to say: "Keep to some topic you understand." Then she dared not say it, for now she could not run the risk of losing her job. She faced him steadily, in angry silence. He left the room, and the little green-tarnished mirror under the pigeonholes saw tears for the first time.

The irony of her position moved her cruelly when she began her task of dealing with the correspondents. Here she was, giving helpful, cheery advice, posing as all-wise in these matters, when her own love affair had come so miserably to grief. In the ill-written scrawls on scented and scalloped paper she could hear an echo of her own suffering. "Hopeless" and "Uncertain" and "Miss Eighteen" got very tender replies that day. And how she laid the lash upon "Beau Brummel" and "Disillusioned," those self-assured young men, who had chosen that mail to contribute their views on the flirtatious and unreliable qualities of modern girls.

The bitterness of her paradoxical task became dulled as the days went on, but there were other troubles, too, to bother her. Her mother, quick and querulous to detect unhappiness, fell into one of her nervous spells, and the doctor had to be called in again. The woman-by-the-day got blood-poisoning in her arm, and could not come. The landlord gave notice of a coming raise in rent. A fat letter came from Arthur, and in a flush of passion she destroyed it unread. If it hadn't been such a fat letter, she said to herself, it wouldn't have annoyed her so to see it. But she wasn't going to wade through pages of explanation of just what he had meant. She was still cut to the quick when she remembered the cavalier and easy way in which he had scoffed at her work. And then, as time went by, she found herself moving into a new mood—no longer one of exaggerated tenderness toward her clients, but a feeling almost cynical. "They're all fools, just as I am," she said.

One morning she found on her desk a note from the managing editor:

Dear Miss Cupid:

We've made some changes in our budget, and I've been authorized to fatten your envelope $15 a week. I'm glad to do this, because the Lovelorn stuff is going big. Just keep kidding them along and everything will be fine. Maybe some day we can syndicate it. Hope this will cheer you up, don't look so blue at your friends.

Sikes.

There had been a time when the tone and phrasing of this note might have seemed offensive, but in the numbness of despondency Ann had felt lately, it was a fine burst of rosy warmth. Thank God, she said to herself, something has broken my way at last! She wondered if she had been mistaken in Sikes, after all? Perhaps he was really a friend of hers, and she had misunderstood his odd ways.

That day at noon she went down to the cashier's department to cash a small check. There was no one in the cage, but in the adjoining compartment, behind a wall of filing cases, she could hear two girls talking. One of them said:

"I see Sikes has put through a raise for Lovelorn. Pretty soft for her, hey?"

"She'll have to give value received, I guess," said the other. "Sikes figures if he puts that over for her, she'll fall for him. She's been stalling him for quite a while, but I suppose he's got her fixed now."

She fled, aghast, ran down to another floor so as not to be seen, and took the elevator. Out on the street she walked mechanically along Park Row and found herself opposite St. Paul's. She wandered in and sat down on a bench. It was a chilly day, and the churchyard was nearly empty.

So this was Sikes's friendliness; and she, utterly innocent even in thought, was already the subject of vulgar office gossip. For the first time there broke in upon her, with bitter force, the knowledge that no matter how easy it may be to counsel others, few of us are wise in our own affairs.

Pitiable paradox: she, the "sympathetic adviser in matters of the heart," had made shipwreck of her own happiness. How right Arthur had been, and how childish and mad she, to reject his just instinct. It was true: she had made use of Love for mere newspaper circulation; and now Love had died between her hands. Well, this was the end. No matter what happened, she could not go on with the job. Cold and trembling with nervousness, she returned to her desk, to finish her column for the next day.

On her typewriter lay some letters, which had come in while she was out. She opened one, and read.

27

Dear Cynthia:

I am in great trouble, please help me. I am in love with a fellow and know he is all right and we would be very happy together. We were engaged to be married, and everything was lovely. But he objected to the work I was doing, said it was not a good job for a girl and that I ought to give it up. I knew he was right, but the way he said it made me mad. I guess I am hot-tempered and stubborn—anyway, I told him to mind his own business, and he went away. Now I am heart-broken, because I love him and I know he loves me. Tell me what to do.

Jessie.

Ann sat looking at the cheap blue paper with the initial J gaudily embossed upon it in gilt. In the sprawling lines of unlettered handwriting she saw an exact parallel to her own unhappy rupture with Arthur. How much more clearly we can see the answer in others' tangles than in our own! Jessie, with her pathetic pretentious gilt initial, knew that she had been in the wrong, and was brave enough to want to make amends. And she—had she not been less true to Love than Jessie? Her false pride and obstinacy had brought their own punishment. Seeing the situation through Jessie's eyes, she could read her duty plain. Arthur, no doubt, was through with her forever, but she must play the game no less.

She put Jessie's letter at the head of the Lovelorn column for the next day. Under it she wrote:

Certainly, dear Jessie, if you feel you were in the wrong, you ought to take the first step toward making up. Probably he was tactless in criticizing you, but I am sure he only did it because he had your true interest at heart. So write him a nice letter and be happy together. Your friend Cynthia hopes it will all come out all right, because she has seen other cases like this where false pride caused great suffering. If he is the right man, he will love you all the more after he gets your letter.

Ann sent up her copy to the composing room, and then going to a telephone booth she called up Fawcett and Company and asked for Mr. Caldwell.

"Mr. Caldwell's not here any longer," said the girl.

"Serves me right," said Ann to herself. "Can you tell me where I can find him?" she asked, wondering how it was that one so miserable could still speak in such a pleasant and apparently unconcerned tone of voice.

The Fawcett operator switched her to another wire.

"I'm sorry," said a stenographer, "Mr. Fawcett left here about two weeks ago. He's got a job out of town—in Boston, I think. I can find out for you in the morning if you'll call again."

"Never mind," said Ann.

She had a horror of facing Mr. Sikes in her present wretchedness, so before she went home she wrote him a note, resigning her job, and asking permission to leave as soon as possible.

The next day she had to nerve herself to face his protests, and the friendly remarks of all the staff when the news spread. It was a hideous ordeal, but she managed to get through it smiling. But by evening she was inwardly a wreck. In her present mood, she had an instinctive longing to revisit the shabby little restaurant where she and Arthur had spent so many happy hours. She knew it would give her pain; but she felt that pain was what she needed—sharp, clean, insistent pain to ease the oppression and disgust of what she had been through. Remorse, she felt, is surgical in action: it cuts away foul tissues of the mind. She could not, without preparatory discipline, face her mother's outcry at hearing she had given up her job.

V

In the crisp blue evening air the bright front of Piazza's café shone with a warm and generous lustre. From sheer force of habit, her heart lightened a little as she climbed the stairs and entered the familiar place, where festoons of red and green paper decoration criss-crossed above the warm, soup-flavoured, tobacco-fogged room. There was a clatter of thick dishes and a clamour of talk.

"One?" said the head waiter, his wiry black hair standing erect as though in surprise.

She nodded, and followed him down the narrow aisle. There was the little table, in the corner under the stair, where they had always sat. A man was there, reading a newspaper.... Her heart felt very strange, as though it had dropped a long way below its usual place. It was Arthur, and he was smiling at her as though nothing had happened. He was getting up. . . he was shaking hands with her. . . how natural it all seemed!

Like all really great crises, it was over in a flash. She found herself sitting at the little table, taking off her gloves in the most casual fashion. Arthur was whispering outrageous things. How fine it is that everybody talks so loud in Italian table d'hôtes, and the waiters crash the dishes round so recklessly!

Arthur's talk seemed to be in two different keys, partly for the benefit of old Tonio, the waiter, and partly for her alone.

"Well, here you are! I wondered how soon you'd get here.... Have you forgiven me, dearest?. . . Do you want some minestrone?. . . Why didn't you answer my letters, brownest eyes? . . . Yes, and some of the near-beer.. . . Darling, it was all my fault. I wrote to tell you so. Didn't you get my letter?"

After all, at such times there isn't much explaining done, A happy reconciliation is the magic of a moment, and no explanations are necessary. The trouble just drops away, and life begins again from the last kind thing that was said. All Ann could do was whisper:

"No, Arthur—it was I who was wrong. I—I've given up the Lovelorn."

And then, after a sudden moisture of eye on both sides, the steaming minestrone came on in its battered leaden tureen from which the silver plating disappeared long ago, and under pretense of serving her soup Arthur stretched out his hand. She put out hers to meet it, and found the ring slipped deftly back on her finger.

"But, Arthur," she said, presently, "I thought you were out of town."

"I was," he said. "I've got a new job, with King and Company in Boston. A good job, too, we can be married right away, and you don't need to worry."

"Well, how did you happen to come here tonight? You didn't know I was going to be here. I didn't know it myself until an hour or so ago."

"Perhaps I willed you to come, who knows?" he said, gaily. "Have you been advising lovers all this while, and didn't know that they always haunt the scenes of former felicity? I've been in town several days, and came here every night."

He produced a copy of the Evening Planet which he had been reading when she came in.

"I had a special reason for thinking you might come here to-night," he said. "This afternoon I read your column, and I saw Jessie's letter and your answer. What you said made me think that perhaps you might be willing to forgive me." Ann, once more safely enthroned on the shining glory of her happiness, felt that she could afford to tease him just a little.

"Ah," she said, "so you admit that some of those letters people write me are genuine, and that the answers do some good?"

He smiled at her and laid his hand over the ring, which outglittered even the most newly nickeled of Piazza's cutlery.

"Yes, honey," he said. "I admit it. And I knew that Jessie's letter was genuine, because I wrote it myself."

THE CURIOUS CASE OF KENELM DIGBY

WE HAD been dining together at the Hotel Ansonia, and as we walked up the shining breezy channel of Broadwhat is the commonest phrase of the detectives? To put two and two together. What else, I ask you, is the poet doing all the time but putting two and two together—two rhymes, and then two rhymes more, and making a quatrain.

He swung his stick, puffed strongly at his cigar, and amorously surveyed the deep blue of the night, against which the huge blocks of apartment houses spread their random patterns of lighted windows. Between these granolithic cliffs flowed a racing stream of bright motors, like the rapids of a river of light hurrying downward to the whirlpool of Times Square.

My friend Dove Dulcet (the well-known poet and literary agent) vigorously expounded a theorem which I afterward had occasion to remember.

"There is every reason," he cried, "why a poet should be the best of detectives! My boy, there is a rhyme in events as well as in words. When you see two separate and apparently unconnected happenings that seem (as one might say) to rhyme together, you begin to suspect one author behind them both. It is the function of the poet to have a quick and tender apprehension of similarities. The root of poetry is nothing else than describing things as being like other apparently quite different things. The lady who compared herself to a bird in a gilded cage was chaffed for her opulent and spendthrift imagination; but in that lively simile she showed an understanding of the poetic principle. Look here:

"Either for a poet or for a detective," he said, gaily, "this seems to me the ideal region. I tell you, I walk about here suspecting the most glorious crimes. When I see the number of banana splits that are consumed in these glittering drugstores, I feel sure that somewhere, in the purple silences of the night, hideous consequences must follow. Those who feed so violently on that brutalizing mixture of banana, chocolate ice cream, cherry syrup, and whipped marshmallow, must certainly be gruesome at heart. I look out of my window late at night toward the scattered lights of that vast pile of apartments, always thinking to see them blaze some great golden

32

symbol or letter into the darkness, some terrible or obscene code that means death and terror."

"Your analogy seems to have some sense," I said. "Certainly the minor poet, like the law breaker, loves to linger about the scene of his rhyme, or crime."

"You are an amateur of puns," he replied. "Then let me tell you the motto I have coined to express the spirit of this Little White Way—Ein feste bourgeois ist unser Gott. This is the proud kingdom of the triumphant middle class. It is a perilous country for a poet. If he were found out, he would be martyred at the nearest subway station. But how I love it! See how the quiet side streets cut across highways so richly contrasting: West End Avenue, leafy, expensive, and genteel; Broadway, so gloriously cruel and artificial; Amsterdam Avenue, so honestly and poignantly real. My club is the Hartford Lunch Room, where they call an omelet an omulet, and where the mystic word Combo resounds through the hatchway to the fat man in the kitchen. My church is the St. Agnes branch of the Public Library, over on Amsterdam Avenue. In those cool, quiet rooms, when I watch the pensive readers, I have a sense of treading near an artery of fine human idealism. In all this various neighbourhood I have a cheerful conviction that almost anything might happen. In the late afternoons, when the crosswise streets end on a glimpse of the Jersey bluffs that glow like smoky blue opals, and smell like rotten apples, I feel myself on the very doorsill of the most stunning outrages."

We both laughed, and turned off on Seventy-seventh Street to the small apartment house where Dulcet had a comfortable suite of two rooms and bath. In his book-lined sitting room we lit our pipes and sat down for a gossip.

We had been talking at dinner of the extraordinary number of grievous deaths of well-known authors that had happened that year. As it is almost unnecessary to remind you, there was Dunraven Bleak, the humorous essayist, who was found stark (in both senses) in his bathtub; and Cynthia Carboy, the famous writer of bedtime stories, who fell down the elevator shaft. In the case of Mrs. Carboy, the police were distracted because her body was found at the top of the building, and the detective bureau insisted that in some unexplainable manner she must have fallen up the shaft; but as Dulcet pointed out at the time of the Authors' League inquiry, the body might have been carried upstairs after the accident. Then there

33

was Andrew Baffle, the psychological novelist, whose end was peculiarly atrocious and miserable, because it seemed that he had contracted tetanus from handling a typewriter ribbon that showed signs of having been poisoned. Frank Lebanon, the brilliant short-story writer, was stabbed in the fulness of his powers; and there were others whom I do not recall at the moment. Mr. Dulcet had suffered severely by these sad occurrences, for a number of these authors were his clients, and the loss of the commissions on the sale of their works was a serious item. The secret of these tragedies had never been discovered, and there had been something of a panic among members of the Authors' League. The rumour of a pogrom among bestselling writers was tactfully hushed.

"What is your friend Kenelm Digby writing nowadays?" I asked, as I looked along Dulcet's shelves. Digby, the brilliant novelist, was probably Dulcet's most distinguished client, an eccentric fellow who, in spite of his excellent royalties, lived a solitary and modest existence in a boardinghouse somewhere in that part of the West Side. Outside his own circle of intimates Dulcet was almost the only man whom Digby saw much of, and many of us, who admired the novelist's work, had our only knowledge of his person from hearing the agent talk of him.

"By George, I'm glad you reminded me," said Dulcet. "Why, he has just finished a story, and he telephoned me this afternoon asking me to stop over at his house this evening to get the manuscript. He never has any dealings with the editors on his own hook—likes me to attend to all his business arrangements for him. I said I'd run over there about ten o'clock."

"That last book of his was a great piece of work," I said. "I've been following his stuff for over ten years, and he looks to me about the most promising fellow we've got. He has something of the Barrie touch, it seems to me."

"Yes, he's the real thing," said Dulcet, blowing a blue cloud of his Cartesian Mixture. "I only wish he were not quite so eccentric. He lives like a hermit-crab, over in a lodging-house near the Park. Even I, who know him as well as most people, never feel like intruding on him except when he asks me to. I can't help thinking it would be good for him to get out more and see something of other men in his line of work. I tried to get him to join The Snails, but he says that Amsterdam Avenue is his only amusement. And Central Park seems to be his country club. I wonder if you've noticed that in his tales

34

whenever he wants to describe a bit of country he takes it right out of the Park. I sometimes suspect that's the only scenery he knows."

"He has attained a very unusual status among writers," I said. "In my rambles among bookshops I have noticed that his first editions bring quite a good price. It's very seldom that a writer—at any rate an American—gets 'collected' during his lifetime."

"Did you ever see any of his manuscript?" asked Dulcet; and on my shaking my head, he took out a thick packet of foolscap from a cabinet.

"This is the original of 'Girlhood'," he explained. "Digby gave it to me. It'll be worth a lot some day."

I looked with interest at the neatly written sheets, thickly covered with a small, beautiful, and rather crabbed penmanship.

"Worth a lot!" I exclaimed. "Well, I should say so! Why the other day I was browsing round in a bookshop and I found a lot of his first editions marked at $15 each. It struck me as a very high price for I know I have seen them listed for three or four dollars in catalogues."

"Exorbitantly high," Dulcet said. "I'm afraid your bookseller is profiteering. I admire Digby as much as any one, but that is an artificial price. The firsts aren't rare enough to warrant any such price as that. Still, I'm glad to know about it as it's a sign of growing recognition. I remember the time when it was all I could do to get any editors to look at his things. I'll have to tell him about that, it will please him mightily."

We sat for a while chatting about this and that and then Dulcet got up and put on his hat.

"Look here, old man," he said. "You squat here and be comfortable while I run round to Digby. It won't take me more than a few minutes—he lives on Eighty-second Street. I'll be back right speedily, and we can go on with our talk." I heard him go down in the elevator, and then I refit my pipe, and picked out a book from one of his shelves. I remember that it was Brillat-Savarin's amusing "Gastronomy as a Fine Art". I smiled at finding this in Dulcet's library, for I knew that the agent rather prided himself on being something of a gourmet, and I was reading the essays of the jovial French epicure with a good deal of relish when the telephone rang. I went to it with that slight feeling of embarrassment one always has in answering someone else's phone.

35

To my surprise, it was Dulcet's voice.

"Hullo?" he said. "That you, Ben? Listen, I want you to come round to Digby's right away," and he gave the address.

Thinking he had arranged a chance for me to meet Digby (I had long wanted to do so), I felt hesitant about intruding; but he repeated his message rather sharply. "Please come at once," he said. "It's important." Again he gave the street number, made me promise to come immediately, and rang off.

It was nearly half-past ten, and the streets were fairly quiet as I walked briskly along. The house was one of a row of old cocoa-coloured stone dwellings, and evidently someone was watching for me, for while I was trying to read the numbers a door opened and from a dark hall an arm beckoned to me. I went up the tall steps and a stout woman, who seemed to be in some agitation, whispered my name interrogatively. "Is this Mr. Trovato?" she murmured.

"Yes," I said, puzzled.

"Third floor front," she said, and I creaked quietly up the stairs.

I tapped at the front room on the top floor, and Dulcet opened.

"Thank goodness you're here, Ben," he said. "Something has happened."

It was a large, comfortable room, crowded with books on three walls, furnished with easy chairs and a couch in one corner. A brilliant blaze of light from several bulbs under a frosted hood poured upon a reading table in the middle of the room. Sitting at this table, in a Windsor chair, slumped down into the seat, was a short stout man whose head lolled sideways over his chest. He was wearing a tweed suit and a soft shirt, and looked as though he had fallen asleep at his work. In front of him were some books and a can of tobacco. I recognized him, of course, from the photographs I had often seen. It was Digby.

I looked at Dulcet, aghast. But, as always at such moments, what was uppermost in my mind was something trivial and irrelevant. I had an intense desire to open a window. The air in that room was thick and foggy, a sort of close, strangling frowst of venomously strong tobacco and furnace gas. After the clear elixir of the wintry night it was loathsome. It was the typical smell that hangs about the rooms of literary bachelors, who work all day long in a room without ever thinking of airing it.

"Yes," he said. "He's dead. Pretty awful, isn't it? I found him like this when I got here. No sign of injury as far as I can see."

There was something profoundly dreadful in this first sight, as mere sagging clay, of the brilliant and powerful writer whose books I had so long admired, and whom I had thought of as one of the strong and fortunate few who shape human perplexities to their own ends. I looked down at him with a miserable blackness in my spirit, and laid a hand on Dulcet's shoulder in sympathy.

"I've sent for a doctor," he said. "Before he comes I want to get all the information I can from the landlady. I wanted to have you here as a witness. I haven't touched anything."

The woman had followed me upstairs, and stood crying quietly in the doorway.

"Come in, Mrs. Barlow," said Dulcet. "Now please tell us everything you can about where Mr. Digby went this evening, and anything that has happened."

Mrs. Barlow, who seemed to be a good-hearted, simple-minded creature, snuffled wretchedly. "Oh, dear, oh dear," she said. "He was such a nice gentleman, too. Let me see, he went out about seven, I suppose for his supper, but he was always irregular about his meals, you never could tell, sometimes he would eat in the middle of the afternoon, and sometimes not till late at night. I always would urge him that he would die of indigestion, but he was so kind-hearted."

"You don't know where he went?" said Dulcet. "Perhaps he went round to the laundry," she said, "for he had a parcel with him, which I took to be his laundry because he usually took it out on Monday evenings because by that time the clean shirt he put on on Sunday was ready to go to the wash. I hate to think that in all the years he lived in this house his laundry was the only thing we ever had a difference about, because I used to have it done in the house for him but he said my washwoman tore the buttons off his shirts or collars or something, so a little while ago he started taking his things out to be done, but I don't know where because he used to call for them himself."

"You haven't any idea where he used to eat?" insisted Dulcet.

"Oh, no, sir, he liked to go different places, you know yourself how he was always a bit queer and concentric and he never talked much about where he went, but always so nice and considerate. Oh, he was a fine gentleman."

Mrs. Barlow, plainly much grieved, wept anew. "Please try to tell us everything you can think of," said Dulcet, gently. "What time did he come in, and did you notice anything unusual?"

"Nothing out of the way that I can think of, but then I was down in the basement most of the evening, for I let my maid go to the movies and I had a deal to do. I suppose he went along Amsterdam Avenue, he was always strolling up and down Amsterdam or Columbus, poor man, getting ideas for his literature I guess. He came back about nine o'clock I should say, because I heard the door about then. Just a few minutes before he came in there was a man came to the door with a tin of tobacco for him, which he said Mr. Digby had ordered sent around, and I took it up and put it on his table, there it is now, poor man, Carter's Mixture."

Mrs. Barlow pointed to the tin of Cartesian Mixture that stood on the table. Evidently it had only just been opened, for it was practically full.

"Yes," said Dulcet. "Here's his pipe lying on the floor under his chair." He picked up the briar and glanced at it. "Only just begun to smoke it, for the tobacco is hardly burned. He must have been smoking when he.... There wasn't anything else you can think of?"

The woman dried her eyes with her apron. "There was just one other thing I noticed, but I suppose it's silly. But I took note of it special, because I thought I had heard it before, lately. While he was out, and a little before the man brought the tin of tobacco, I heard a sharp tapping out on the street in front of the house. I noticed it special, because I thought at first it was someone rapping on the door, and I wondered if the bell was out of order again, but when I went I couldn't see any one. But I wondered about it because I heard it two or three times, a sharp kind of tapping, it sounded some way like hitting on stone with a stick of some sort."

Dulcet and I looked at each other rather blankly.

"And after that," she went on, "I didn't think about anything one way or another till you came in and I told you to go right up."

There was a clear peal from the front door bell. "That's the doctor," said Dulcet, and Mrs. Barlow hurried downstairs.

I have never seen any one so brisk and matter of fact as that physician, and after his arrival the affair seemed to pass out of Dulcet's hands into the painful official machinery that takes charge in such events. Dulcet, acting as the dead writer's literary representative, went into the adjoining room, which was Digby's study, to look over the papers in the desk for any manuscripts that he ought to take care of. He wrote out a list of friends and relatives for me to send telegrams to and I went out to attend to this. I don't know how they get wind of these affairs, but the reporters were already beginning to arrive when I left.

The next day, and for several days afterward, the papers all carried long stories about poor Digby's brilliant career. Then the literary weeklies took it up. At the libraries and bookshops everyone was asking for his books, and I have never seen a more depressing illustration of the familiar fact that a writer's real fame never comes until it is too late to do him any good. Editors and people who had hardly been aware of Digby's genius while he was alive now praised him fluently, speaking of him as "America's most honest realist," and all that sort of thing. Moving-picture people began inquiring about the film rights of his novels. Some of the sensational newspapers tried to play up his death as a mystery story, but the physicians asserted heart failure as the cause, and this aspect of the matter soon subsided.

Except at the funeral, which was attended by a great many literary people, I did not see Dulcet for some days. I gathered from what I read in the news that Digby's will had appointed him executor of his literary property, and I knew that he must have much to attend to. But one afternoon the telephone rang, and Dulcet asked me if I could knock off work and come round to see him. As I was living up town at that time, it only took me a few minutes to go round to his apartment. I found him smoking a pipe as usual, and looking pale and fagged. He welcomed me with his affectionate cordiality, and I sat down to hear what was on his mind.

"You must excuse me if I'm a little upset," he said. "I've just had an interview with a ghoul. A fellow came in to see me who had heard that I have a number of poor Digby's books and manuscripts. He wanted to buy them from me, offered big prices for them. He said that since Digby's death all his first editions and so on have gone up enormously in value. Apparently he expected me to do trading over the dead body of a friend."

He smoked awhile in silence, and then said: "Sorry not to have seen you sooner, but to tell the truth I've had my hands full. His brother, who was the nearest kin, couldn't come from Ohio on account of serious illness, and everything fell on me. I had to pack up all his things and ship them, all that sort of business. But I've been wanting to talk to you about it, because I'm convinced there was something queer about the whole affair. I'm not satisfied with that heart-failure verdict. That's absurd. There was nothing wrong with his heart that I ever heard of. It's very unfortunate that for the first few days I was too occupied with urgent matters to be able to follow up the various angles of the affair. But I've been turning it over in my mind, and I've got some ideas I'd like to share with you. You remember what I told you, with unfortunate levity, about the secret of detective work being ability to notice the unsuspected rhymes in events? Well, there are one or two features of this affair that seem to me to rhyme together in a very sinister fashion. Wait a minute until I put on my other coat, and we'll go out."

He went into his bedroom. I had not liked to interrupt him, but I was yearning for a smoke, for leaving my rooms in a hurry I had forgotten to bring my pouch with me. On his mantelpiece I saw a tin of tobacco, and began to fill my pipe. To my surprise, just as I was taking out a match he darted out of the bedroom, uttered an exclamation, and snatched the briar from my hand.

"Sorry," he said, bluntly, "but you mustn't smoke that. It's something very special." He opened his penknife, scraped out the weed I had put in the bowl, and carefully put it back in the tin. He took the tin and locked it in his desk.

"Try some of this," he said, handing his pouch. I concluded that the tension of the past days had troubled his nerves. This rudeness was so unlike him that I knew there must be some explanation, but he offered none. As we went down in the elevator he said: "The question is, can you make a rhyme out of tobacco and collar buttons?"

"No," I said, a little peevishly. "And I don't believe any one could, except Edward Lear."

"Well," he continued, "that's what we've got to do. And don't imagine that it's merely a nonsense rhyme, any more than Lear's were. Edward Lear was as great as King Lear, in his own way." He led me to Eighty-second Street. The December afternoon was already dark as we approached Mrs. Barlow's house. At the foot of her front steps he halted and turned to me.

"Is your pipe going?" he said.

"No," I said, irritably. "It's out. And I haven't any tobacco."

"Don't be surly, old chap; I'll give you some if you'll tell me what you do when your pipe goes out."

"Why, you idiot," I cried, "I do this." And I knocked out the ashes by striking the bowl smartly against the palm of my hand.

"Ah," he said. "But some people do this."

He bent down and rapped his pipe against the stone ramp of the steps, with a clear, sharp, hollow sound.

"Yes, a good way to break a nice pipe," I was remarking, when the basement door of the house flew open, and Mrs. Barlow darted out into the sunken area just below the pavement level. In the pale lemon-coloured glare of a near-by street lamp we could see that she was strongly excited.

"Good gracious," she panted. "Is it Mr. Dulcet? Oh, sir, you did give me a turn. Oh, dear, that was just the tapping sound I heard the night poor Mr. Digby died. What was it? Did you hear it?"

"Like this?" said Dulcet, knocking his pipe again on the stone step.

"That was it, exactly," she said. "What a fright, to be sure! Was it only someone knocking his pipe like that? Oh, dear, it did bring back that horrid evening, just as plain."

"So much for the mysterious death rap," said Dulcet as we walked back toward Amsterdam Avenue. "I can't claim much ingenuity for that, however. You see, the morning after Digby's death I went round to Mrs. Barlow's early, before she had been out to sweep her pavement. The first thing I noticed, by the lowest step, was a little dottle of tobacco such as falls from a halfsmoked pipe when it is knocked out. That seemed to me to make a perfect couplet with Mrs. Barlow's tale of the tapping she had heard. She heard it several times, you remember, in a short space of time. That suggests to me someone standing on the street, or walking up and down, in a state

41

of nervousness, because he didn't smoke any of his pipes through. When they were only half smoked he knocked them out, in sheer impatience. Was he waiting for someone?"

"Perhaps it was Digby himself?" I suggested. "I don't think so," he said. "Because, in the first place, nervousness was the last thing I would associate with his temperament, which was calm and collected in the extreme. And also, he always smoked Brown Eyed Blend, and had done so for years. That was the first thing that struck me as unusual the night we were there—that tin of Cartesian on the table. He was a man of fixed habits; why should he have made a change just that night? I picked up the little wad of tobacco I found lying on the step, and took it carefully home. It's Cartesian, or I'm a Dutchman. So item I in our criminal rhyme-scheme is: Find me a nervous man smoking Cartesian."

"It's a bit fanciful," I objected.

"Of course it is," he cried. "But crime is a fanciful thing. Ever let the fancy roam, as Keats said. What the deuce is the line that follows? Suppose we stroll down Amsterdam Avenue and find a new place to have dinner."

"Poor old Digby," he said, as we walked along admiring the lighted caves of the shopwindows. "How he enjoyed all this. You know, there is a certain honest simplicity about Amsterdam Avenue's merchandising that is pleasant to contemplate after the shining sophistications of Broadway. In a Broadway delicatessen window you'll see such horrid luxuries as jars of cocks' combs in jelly; whereas along here the groceries show candid and heartening signs such, as this: 'Coming Back to The Old Times, 17c lb. Sugar.' Amsterdam Avenue shopkeepers speak with engaging directness about their traffic; for instance, there's a barber at the corner of Eighty-first Street who embosses on his window the legend: 'Yes, We Do Buster Brown Hair Cutting.' That sort of thing is very humane and genuine, that's why Digby was so fond of it. There's a laundry along here somewhere that I have often noticed; it calls itself the Fastidious Laundry——"

"Speaking of laundries," I said, "what do you think of this?" We stopped, and I pointed to a neatly lettered placard in a window which had caught my eye. It said:

Notice to Artists and Authors

"By Jove," I said, "there's a laundry that has the right idea. I think I'll bring my——"

I broke off when I saw my companion's face. He was leaning forward toward the pane, and his eyes were bright but curiously empty, as though in some way the mechanism of sight had been reversed, and he was looking inward rather than out.

"That's very odd," he said, presently. "I've been up and down this street many times, but I never noticed that sign before."

He turned and marched into the shop, and I followed. In the soft steamy air several girls were ironing shirts, and a plump, pink-cheeked Hebrew stood behind a counter wrapping up bundles.

"I noticed your sign in the window," said Dulcet. "What do you charge for laundering soft collars?"

"Five cents each, but we mend them, too, and sew on the buttons."

"That's a good idea," said Dulcet, genially. "I wish I'd known that before; I'd have brought my collars round to you. How long have you been doing that? I often go by here, but I never saw the sign before."

"Only about a week," the man replied. "Let's see—a week ago last Monday I put that sign up. You wouldn't believe how much new trade it has brought in. I thought it would be a kind of a joke—the man next door suggested it, and I put it in to please him. But 'most everybody wears soft collars nowadays, and it seems good business."

"The man next door?" said Dulcet, in a casual tone.

"Sure, the cigar store."

"Is his name Stork?" said Dulcet, reflectively.

"Stork? Why, no, Basswood. What do you mean, Stork?"

"I mean," said Dulcet, slowly, "does he ever stand on one leg?"

"Quit your kidding," cried the laundryman, annoyed.

43

"I assure you, I do not trifle," said Dulcet, gravely. "I'll bring you in some collars to fix up for me. Much obliged."

We went out again, and my companion stood for a moment in front of the laundry window, looking thoughtfully at the sign.

"While you ponder, old son," I said, "I'll run into Mr. Stork-Basswood's and get some tobacco."

He seized my arm in a firm and painful clutch and whispered, "Look at the corner!"

The laundry was the second shop from the corner. Under the lamp-post at the angle of the street I saw, to my amazement, a man standing balanced on one leg. Directly under the light, he was partly in shadow, and I could only see him in silhouette, but the absurd profile of his onelegged attitude afflicted me with a renewed sense of absurdity and irritation. Dulcet, I thought, had evidently suffered some serious stroke in the region of his wits.

"Now," he said, softly, "can you see any rhyme between soft collars and standing on one leg?"

As he spoke, we both started, for somewhere near us on the street there sounded a sharp tapping, a ringing hollow wooden sound. Evidently it came from the one-legged man. This was too much for my composure. I broke away from Dulcet and ran to the corner. As I got there the one-legged creature put down a concealed limb and stood solidly on two feet, in a state of normalcy, as an eminent statesman would say. I was confused, and said angrily to the man:

"Here, you mustn't stand like that, on the public street you know, on one leg. It's setting a bad example."

To my amazement he made no retort whatever, but turned and scuttled hastily down the avenue, disappearing in the crowds that were doing their evening marketing.

"My dear fellow," said Dulcet, calmly, coming up to me, "you shouldn't have done that. You've very nearly spoilt it all. Come on, let's go in and get your tobacco."

Basswood's proved to be one of those interesting combination tobacco, stationery, toy, and bookshops which are so common on the upper West Side. I have often noticed that these places are by no means unfruitful as hunting ground for books, because the dealers

44

are wholly ignorant of literature and sometimes one may find on their shelves some forgotten volume that has been there for years, and which they will gladly part with for a song. A good many of these stores have, tucked away at the back, a shabby stock of circulating library volumes that have come down through many changes of proprietorship. Only the other day I saw in just such a place first editions of Kenneth Grahame's "The Golden Age" and Arthur Machen's "The Three Impostors," which the storekeeper was delighted to sell for fifteen cents each.

A dark young man was behind the tobacco counter, and from him I got a packet of my usual blend.

"Mr. Basswood in?" said Dulcet.

"Just stepped out," said the young man.

We lit our pipes and looked round the shop, glancing at the magazines and the queer miscellany of books. As it was approaching Christmas time there was a profuse assortment of those dreadful little bibelots that go by the name of "gift books," among which were the usual copies of "Recessional" and "Vampire," Thoreau's "Friendship," and "Ballads of a Cheechako," bound in what the trade calls "padded ooze". I was particularly heartened to observe that one of these atrocities, called "As a Man Thinketh," was described on the box (for all such books come in little cardboard cases) as being bound in antique yap. This pleased me so much that I was about to call it to Dulcet's attention, when I saw that he was looking at me from the rear of the store with a spark in his eye. I approached and found that he was staring at a doorway partly concealed by a pile of Christmas toys and novelties. Over this door was a sign: J. Basswood, Rare Book Department.

"Can we go in and look at the rare books?" said Dulcet.

"Sure thing," said the young man. "Help yourself. The boss'll be back soon, if you want to buy anything."

Mr. Basswood was evidently a man of some literary discretion. To our amazement we found, in a dark little room lined with shelves, a judicious assortment of modern books, several hundred volumes, and all first editions or autographed copies. The prices were marked in cipher, so we could not tell whether there were any bargains among them, but I know that I saw several particularly rare and desirable things which I would have been glad to have.

45

"Good heavens," I said to Dulcet, "friend Basswood is a real collector. There isn't a thing here that isn't of prime value."

He was staring at a shelf in the corner, and I went over to see what he had found.

"Upon my soul," I cried, "look at the Digbies! Not merely one copy of each, but three or four! This man must have specialized in Digbies."

"Not only that," said Dulcet, "but he has three of 'The Autogenesis of a Novelist', the first thing that Digby wrote. It was privately printed, and afterward suppressed. It's devilish rare; even I haven't got a copy. I wish I knew what prices he asks for these things."

"Look at this," I said. "Perhaps this will tell us." I picked up one of a pile of pamphlets that were lying in a large sheet of wrapping paper in a corner of the room. It was evidently a new catalogue of Mr. Basswood's rare books, that had just come from the printer.

"Here we are," I said, turning over the leaves. "Look at this."

Special Note

Fine Collection of Digbiana: J. Basswood wishes to call particular attention to the Digbiana listed below. Anticipating the growing interest in collectors' items of this great writer's work, J. Basswood has taken pains to gather a stock of first editions and presentation copies which is absolutely unique. The prices of these items, while high, are a fair index of the appreciation in which this author's work is held among connoisseurs. All are copies in good condition and their authenticity is guaranteed.

November 15, 19—.

Dulcet seized the catalogue and ran his eye down the pages.

"'Girlhood,' first edition, Houghton Mifflin Company, 1901, $100," he read. "'The Nuisance of Being Loved,' first edition, $75. 'The Princess Quarrelsome,' $90. 'The Anatomy of Cheerfulness,' autographed copy, $150. 'Distemper,' acting copy, signed by the author and Richard Mansfield, $200.

"Why," he cried, shrilly, "this is madness! I am in touch with all the dealers in this sort of thing, and I know the proper prices. This man has multiplied them by ten." He thrust the catalogue into his pocket and glared round at the musty shelves.

"I suppose it's due to poor Digby's death," I said. I saw that Dulcet was overwrought, and suggested that we go out and get some supper.

"Supper?" he said. "A good idea. I know a place on Broadway where we can get some guinea pigs." He strode out of the store and I followed, wondering what next. He seized my arm and hurried me along Seventy-ninth Street to Broadway.

In the clarid blue of the evening that blazing gully of light seemed to foam and bubble with preposterous fire. Chop suey restaurants threw out crawling streamers of red and yellow brilliance; against the peacock green of the western sky the queer church at the corner of Seventy-ninth, with the oriental pinnacle and truncated belfry rising above its solid Baptist wings, seemed like the offspring of some reckless marriage of two infatuated architects, one Jewish and one Calvinist. It was a fitting silhouette, I thought, congruent with an evening of such wild humours. Guinea pigs for supper, how original and enlivening! "Are guinea pigs properly kosher?" I asked, sarcastically.

Dulcet paid no heed, but, holding my arm, urged me along the pavement to an animal shop on the western side of Broadway. The window was full of puppies and long-haired cats. All down the aisle of the establishment were tiers of birdcages, covered with curtains while the birds slept. In lucid bowls persevering goldfish pursued their glittering and improfitable round.

"Those guinea pigs I ordered," said Dulcet to the man, "are they ready?"

"All ready, sir," he said, and took out a cage from under the counter. "Very fine pigs, sir, strong and hearty; they will stand a great deal."

"Yes," I said, with a wild desire to shout with laughter. "But will they stand being eaten? They will find that rather trying, I fancy."

Dulcet tapped his forehead, and the dealer smiled indulgently. My companion took the cage, paid some money, and sped outdoors again.

I made no further comment and in a few minutes we were in Dulcet's apartment.

"You have no kitchenette here, have you?" I protested. "Or do we devour them raw? Oh, I see, you have a camp oven. How ingenious!"

He had put on the table a large tin box. With complete seriousness he now produced a small spirit lamp, over which he fitted a little basket of fine wire mesh. When the flame of the lamp was lit, it played upon the basket, which was supported by legs at just the right height. He now put the unsuspecting guinea pigs into the tin box, which was shaped like a rural-free-delivery letter-box, with a hinged door opening at one end. He took the spirit lamp with its attached basket and pushed the contraption carefully into the box with the pigs. Then he opened both windows in the room.

"Admirable!" I exclaimed. "Like those much-advertised cigarettes, they will be toasted. But won't it take a long time?"

"Don't be an ass," he said.

He went to his desk, and took out the tin of Cartesian Mixture he had snatched away from me earlier in the evening.

"Your mention of those cigarettes is apt," he said, "for in this case also the fuel is tobacco. Please go over by the window, and stay there."

I watched, somewhat impressed by the gravity of his manner. From the tin of tobacco he took a small pinch of mixture and carefully placed it in the mesh basket above the lamp. Reaching into the box, he lit the wick of the lamp with a match, and hastily clapped to the hinged lid. The guinea pigs seemed to be awed by these proceedings, for they remained quiet. Dulcet joined me at the window, and remarked that fresh air was a fine thing.

We waited for about five minutes, while the guinea-pig oven stood quietly on the table.

"Well," said Dulcet, finally, "we ought to be able to see whether it rhymes or not."

He snatched open the door of the tin box, and skipped away from it in a way that seemed to me perfectly insane. He picked up a pair of tongs from the fireplace, and standing at a distance, lifted out the lamp. The tobacco was smoking strongly in its mesh basket. Holding the lamp away from him with the tongs, he carried it into the bathroom, and I heard him turn on the water. Then, coming back, he inserted the tongs into the tin box, and gingerly withdrew first one guinea pig and then the other. Both were calm as possible, quite dead. Looking over the sill to see that the pavement was clear, he threw the tin box into the street, where it fell with a crash.

"Surely they're not cooked already?" I said.

"I haven't heard from the doctor yet," he said; "but he promised to ring me up this evening. I'm awfully sorry to have delayed your dinner, old man. Meet me at the Lucerne grill room, Seventy-ninth and Amsterdam Avenue, to-morrow evening at seven o'clock and we'll eat together. You've been a great help to me."

"I hope the doctor is a mental specialist," I said; but he pushed me gently out of the room. "We'll finish our rhyme at dinner to-morrow evening."

I went out into the night, and sorrowfully visited a Hartford Lunch.

The next evening I was at the Lucerne grill promptly. This modest chop house was one of Dulcet's favourite resorts, and I found him already sitting in one of the alcoves studying the menu. He was in fine spirits, and his quizzical blue eyes shone with a healthy lustre.

"Are you armed?" he said, mysteriously.

"What," I cried, "are we going to do some more guinea pigs to death? It was cruel. I have scruples against taking innocent lives. Besides, your experiment proved nothing. Those pigs would have died anyway, shut up in an air-tight box like that."

"Stuff!" he said. "The box was not hermetic. I had left small apertures: there was plenty of oxygen. No, it was not the confinement in the tin box that killed them. After you had gone, the chemist whom I had consulted called me up. My suspicions were sound. Have you ever heard of fumacetic acid?"

This is going to be terrible, I thought to myself, and ordered tenderloin steak, well done, with a double order of hashed brown potatoes.

"Have you ever heard of fumacetic acid?" he repeated, relentlessly.

"No," I said, nervously.

49

"It is a deadly and little-known drug," he said, "which (so the chemist tells me) possesses the property that when vaporized the slightest whiff of it causes instant death if inhaled into the lungs. The tobacco in that tin had been doctored with it. I sent the chemist the pipe that poor Digby was smoking when he died, and he analyzed what was left in the bowl. There is no doubt whatever. He was poisoned in that way. I tell you, my professional duty as a literary agent requires that in my clients' interest I should sift this thing to the bottom. It may explain some of those earlier deaths that baffled the Authors' League."

"But Mrs. Carboy, surely, did not smoke," I was about to say; but I checked myself in time.

"Dove," I said, "you are superb. But I wish you would tell me how you worked the thing out. What was it that first aroused your suspicions? If it had not been for you, I should never have guessed anything wrong."

"Of course," he said, grimly, "it was that murderous placard in the laundry window, and that is to your credit, for you noticed it. That was the one thing that made plain the whole complicated business. Naturally I suspected the tobacco from the first, for (as I told you) it was a mixture that Digby never smoked ordinarily. But when I heard that that eccentric and damnable placard had been put there at the suggestion of the tobacconist next door, and then found that the tobacconist was also a bookseller, I knew the worst. I have spent to-day in rounding up the threads, and I think I may say without vainglory that the miscreant is in my power."

"But the man standing on one leg?" I said, puzzled. "What was he up to, and why did he run?" Dulcet's face shone with quiet triumph.

"I told you," he said, "to look for a nervous man smoking Cartesian Mixture. That tobacconist, Basswood, smokes Cartesian. It is a very moist, sticky blend, as you know. It can only be shaken out of the pipe, after smoking, by vigorously knocking the bowl on something hard. Very well, and if there is no stone step or something of that sort handy, what will a smoker tap his pipe on? Why, he will stand on one leg and knock it out on the lifted heel of the other. And his running away when you addressed him so whimsically, wasn't that a pretty good sign of nervousness—and also of a guilty and doubtful spirit?"

He finished his tumbler of the near-beer that has made Milwaukee infamous, and leaned forward earnestly.

"You know very well," he said, "that that laundryman would never have thought of his grotesque notice, addressed to 'Artists and Authors', if someone hadn't suggested it to him. Obviously he was only a gull. That card was intended as a decoy, to lure Digby away from his room, so that Basswood could leave the poisoned tobacco for him. Basswood had studied Digby's habits, and must have known that the notice about the collars would be sure to catch his eye. Now we had better be going. The police will be at Basswood's shop at eight o'clock."

I could have done with a little strong coffee, but he haled me out of the restaurant, and we walked up Amsterdam Avenue. How little, I reflected, did the passersby, hurrying about their kindly and innocent concerns, suspect our dark and perilous errand.

"The motive, of course," said Dulcet, "was to profit by the increase of value Digby's death would give to his literary work. You will see a proof of that in a moment. Here we are. Come on, this is no time to hang back!"

He strode into the brightly lighted shop, and I followed with a clumsy assumption of carelessness. I must confess that my eye wandered in search of suitable cover in case there should be any gun play.

Mr. Basswood was behind his counter, smoking a battered-looking briar. One side of the bowl was worn down nearly half an inch (from repeated knocking out on stone steps, I suppose). He was a fat, cross-looking person, with a black jut of moustache and a small, vindictive eye.

"A friend told me about your bookshop," said Dulcet. "He said that you sometimes buy books and manuscripts and that sort of thing."

"Yes, sometimes," said Basswood, without enthusiasm.

"I have an unpublished story of Kenelm Digby's," said Dulcet. "It is about forty pages of manuscript. What would you give for that?"

The dealer's eyes brightened. He took his pipe from his mouth, and knocked it out smartly on his heel, tramping on the glowing cinders. Dulcet looked at me gravely.

"Let me see it," Basswood said, eagerly.

51

"I haven't got it with me. But give me an idea what it would be worth to you."

"If it is genuine, and characteristic of Digby's genius," said Basswood, slowly, "I would give you two hundred dollars for it."

"Nonsense!" said Dulcet. "It isn't worth half that. I would not dream of selling it for more than seventy-five."

Basswood looked startled.

"I guess you are not in touch with the market for such things," he said. "There is more interest among collectors in Digby's work than in any other recent writer. Perhaps you don't realize what a difference his sad death has made in the prices of his editions. It is very regrettable, but the death of a writer of that kind always puts a premium on collectors' items, because there will never be any more of them."

"Oh, I see," said Dulcet, politely. "It is his death that has made the difference, is it?"

"Exactly."

"Well, then, I suppose this manuscript is worth more than I thought. By the way, I think the title of it will interest you. It is called 'The Mystery of the Soft Collars' and deals with a murder that took place on Eighty-second Street."

I couldn't help admiring the glorious nonchalance with which Dulcet made this remark, gazing the dealer straight in the eye. Basswood's face was a study, and his cheek was pale and greasy. But he, too, was a man of considerable nerve.

"I don't believe it's genuine," he said. "That doesn't sound to me like Digby's style." His voice shook a little, and he added: "However, if it's as interesting as it sounds, I might pay even more than two hundred for it."

"You rascal!" shouted Dulcet. "Do you think you can buy me off? No! keep your hands above the counter!"

He had whipped out his revolver, and held it at the man's face.

"Look here, Mr. Basswood," he said. "Even the cleverest of us make mistakes. Let me call your attention to one thing. If it was Digby's

52

death that made the difference in the values of his books, how is it that this bill from your printer, for that new catalogue of yours, is dated ten days before Digby died? I picked it up in your back room the other day. Doesn't that seem to show that you knew, ten days before the event, that there was going to be a sudden boom in Digbiana? Ten days before he died you were multiplying the prices of the items you had gathered. Now, you dog, can you explain that?"

Basswood shook, but still he clung to his hope.

"I'll give you a thousand for that manuscript," he said.

"Ben," said Dulcet to me, "just slip around the corner and whistle three times. The police are waiting on Eighty-fifth Street."

"There's still one thing that puzzles me," I said to Dulcet late that night as we sat in his room for a final smoke. "I remember that before we discovered that sign in the laundry you said that what we needed to do was to find a rhyme between tobacco and collar buttons. Now what the deuce started you off on collar buttons?"

He smiled patiently.

"When I had to pack up poor old Digby's belongings," he said, "I had the sad task of going through his bureau drawers. You know the devilish little buttons that the manufacturers insist on putting on soft collars. They always come off after one or two washings, and then the collar collapses round your neck into an object of slovenly reproach. Digby was a bachelor, and there was no one to do any mending for him. And when I found that every one of his soft collars had its little button neatly sewed on, I knew there was something wrong. I ask you, wouldn't that have aroused the alarm of the least suspicious?"

Up to the present time, as far as I know, Basswood remains the only bookseller who has ever been electrocuted.

GLORIA AND THE GARDEN OF SWEDEN

IT WAS one of those gilded October days when the serene sunshine is as soft and tawny as candle-light; when the air is thin and sharp in the early mornings, but the noontime is as comfortably genial as the radiance of a hearth reddened with hickory embers. Dove Dulcet and I were strolling along Riverside Park, enjoying the blue elixir of the afternoon, in which there was just a faint prick, a gently tangible barb of the coming arrows of the North.

"Winter sharpens her spearheads," said Dulcet. "Aye," was my reply. Below us I saw the coaling-station at the Seventy-ninth Street pier. "The merriest music the householder can hear nowadays is the roar of coal going down the chute into the cellar."

He sighed, and seemed touched by a sudden melancholy.

"Ben," he said, "that coal-dump reminds me of Gloria Larsen. Did I ever tell you about her?"

"Never," I said. "Coal, I presume, made you think of diamonds; and diamonds, of Miss Larsen. Were you engaged to her?"

"I might have been," he said, sentimentally. Before us was an empty bench, on a little knoll that looks out over the shining sweep of the river. I drew him to it, and we filled our pipes. When you can get a minor poet in an autobioloquacious mood, it is well to encourage him. No one takes life so seriously as the minor poet, and consequently his memoirs make fine sport for the disinterested bystander.

"No," he said, blowing a waft of tobacco smoke into the soft, sun-brimmed air, and settling down into the curve of the bench. "The association was even more obvious than that of coal and diamonds. I always think of Gloria when winter begins to come in."

"Ah!" I said. "She was cold?"

He meditated, ignoring my jocularity.

"It was a good many years ago," he said at last; "before you knew me. When I first came to town, you know, I had a fine ambition to be a writer. I had just a little money, so I shut myself up in a hall room at the top of a cheap lodging-house on Seventy-fifth Street, hired a typewriter, and set about to butt my bead against all the walls that hem in the beginner.

"It was one of those old four-story dwellings that are now mostly boarding-houses, and it was run by a good-hearted widow who would let her rooms only to men, because she said they were less trouble than women. Her house was clean and incredibly cheap, and almost all the lodgers were young fellows like myself—students, or starveling artists, or chaps with literary ambitions. That was how I had heard of the place, through another fellow who lived there and had built up a little sort of coterie in the house. He was Black-more. You know his name; he gave up art long ago. He's now the art editor of the Mother, Home, and Heaven Magazine.

"Mrs. Vesey, our landlady, was quite a character. I was always rather a favourite with her, because the very first day I came to her house I happened to find her cat, which had wandered away some days before, leaving her disconsolate. The cat's name, I remember, was Nemo. She had called it so because, with that admirable virginity of mind that one finds only in a childless married woman, she was uncertain of the animal's sex. Anyway, it was a fine big creature, and the apple of Mrs. Vesey's pie. She talked so much about it that we used to chaff her a good deal on the subject, and say that we thought it was going to have kittens, and all that sort of thing. Blackmore used to say, remembering the title of some idiotic melodrama he had seen, that it was 'Neither Maid, Wife, nor Widow.' He was right, for it was the kind of cat that is not likely to be either a father or a mother without a miracle. But I don't want to be indelicate. I only mention Nemo because it was through him that I first talked with Gloria.

"The first day I was at Mrs. Vesey's I heard her groaning about the vanished cat. That evening I went out to supper, feeling rather lonely, and dropped in at an eccentric-looking little restaurant on Amsterdam Avenue. It was called Larsen's Physical Culture Chophouse, and I have never seen a more amusing place. Old man Larsen was a Swede, and all the Scandinavian fads ran riot in his head—vegetarian food, for instance. He didn't absolutely condemn meat, for he would serve it if you insisted, but all his joy was in weird combinations of calory, protose, and vitamine, or whatever those things are called. Bean "cutlets," and protose "steak" that turned out, on examination, to be made of chopped walnuts and lentils, and the "Thousand-Calory Combination Dinner," of which he made a specialty. When you sat down, if you were a regular customer, old Larsen would come round and look you over and diagnose from your complexion the kind and quantity of calories you needed for that meal, and would give you combinations of spinach croquettes and lentil pie that he warranted would purge the blood and compose the mind. On the walls were charts of Swedish exercises and systems of calisthenics, and he sold a little pamphlet that he himself had written telling how to be strong and merry and full of physique.

"Well, to come back to my first visit to Larsen's restaurant. I hadn't been in there many minutes before I noticed the girl at the cashier's desk. My, my, what a girl! My table was close to her little throne, and I couldn't help watching her out of the end of my eye. I wondered if she was raised entirely on protose and lentils, for I have never seen anything so gloriously and vitally physical in my life. Great, bold blue eyes, and crisp, sparkling golden hair, and blood that spoke delicately through her skin, and a figure—well, just our old friend of Melos over again, that lively combination of grace and strength. She was just curves and waves and athletic softness—the kind of creature that makes your arms tingle, you know. No corset, I suppose. In the old man's booklet on physical culture he defended the gymnastic doctrine that women should develop what he called a muscle corset by bending and swaying from the hips a thousand times a day. He said it must be done—well, au naturel, in front of an open window in one's bedroom in the morning. I'd be ashamed to admit that we fellows at Mrs. Vesey's used to set our alarm clocks at half-past six to go round the corner to Amsterdam Avenue——"

Dulcet paused a while and watched the river pensively.

"But about the cat," I reminded him presently.

"Yes," he said. "Well, that first night I was at the chop-house I noticed a very fine, fat cat browsing about under the tables. I was amused at the corpulence of the animal. I said to myself that a cat as large as that must surely get some meat somewhere, because, while vegetarian protose food may be all right for Swedes, a cat is a realist in the matter of carnal meals. And when I went to the desk to pay my check, wanting some excuse to get into talk with the superb Gloria—who was, of course, the old man's daughter—I remarked on the sleek, healthy appearance of her cat.

"'Oh, it's not ours,' she said. 'It came in here yesterday. I don't know whose he is.'

"I'll bet I know whose it is," I said.

I told her that Mrs. Vesey, who ran the bachelor lodging-house on Seventy-Fifth Street, had lost her Nemo. She listened with interest, those thrilling blue eyes sizing me up in a keen, humorous way.

"'I shouldn't wonder it's hers,' she said.

"Welcoming any pretext for prolonging the discussion, I borrowed the phone at Gloria's elbow, and, studying the heart-rending curves of her chin and cheek and throat, I called up Mrs. Vesey and told her I thought I had found her pet. Mrs. Vesey hurried round to the restaurant, and swept up the vagabond Nemo with cries of joy into her lean and affectionate bosom. Nemo purred, and I escorted Mrs. Vesey home, recapitulating in my mind the perfect contours of the girl's heavenly form. My enthusiasm was even such that when the other men came in I could not refrain from telling them all about her. I saw that I had made a mistake, for instantly Blackmore swore he would get her to sit for him.

"Of course, from that time on, the Physical Culture Chophouse became the nightly haunt of our little party. The other men had seen it many times, but the vegetarian threats in the window had frightened them away. But now, none of us dared to be absent very many dinners, for fear the rest would gain some advantage with the girl. I cannot give you any conception of the humorous glamour of that time unless I insist that she was the most superbly luscious thing I have ever glimpsed; and one sees a good many covetable creatures on the streets of New York. Some of them said she was cold; that in spite of all the nutritious algebra printed on old Larsen's menus (he used to put down all sorts of preposterous formulas about starch, and albumen, and phosphorus, and proteids, and so on)—she was lacking in calories. But I know that when we sat at table, and she came round to ask if everything was all right, and leaned over us with her clear eyes, as blue as a special-delivery stamp, and that cream-white neck, and the faint glimmer of a blue ribbon shining through the hilly slopes of her blouse——-Oh, well, Ben, we were young, and we ate red meat for lunch, anyway.

"I guess old man Larsen, who spent most of his time in the kitchen, encouraged her to kid us along, for he never seemed to mind our open admiration of his daughter. He probably saw that she was a bigger business asset than any number of calory charts. Every now and then he would come out and chin with us, for our party became a nightly event in the café. Before long we had sampled every kind of vegetarian combination on the list, and had him busy inventing new ones. We used to ask him if he had raised a girl like that on nothing but vegetables, and he would laugh and swear that Gloria had never tasted blood until she was sixteen. It seemed queer to us that the restaurant wasn't full of her suitors. I should have thought, with a girl like her, they'd have been standing in line waiting for a look at her. I suppose that people who feed on nothing but vegetables are rather puny in such matters. It's an odd thing, but I've always noticed that most of the people who frequent these crank physical-culture and dietetic eating-places are a queer, sick-looking lot—youths with rolling Adam's apples, and sallow, soup-stained girls. Certainly our little gang, so very jovial and fancy-free, made a quaint contrast to most of the patrons of the house. In a few days we felt as if we owned the place, and had the old man slide two tables together just underneath Gloria's cash register, where we met every evening for dinner.

"As for Larsen, he was a crank on many subjects but he was no fool. He was an athletic, erect fellow with a bristling gray moustache and cropped hair and a forcible gray eye. On the wall was a huge photo of him in a kind of Sandow pose, with a leopard-skin apron round his middle, showing terrific knotty biceps and back muscles. Gloria told us that at one time he had been a physical instructor in the Swedish army, and the head of a Turnverein, or something of that sort. There was a certain physical and gymnastic candour about him that amused us. He was awfully proud of Gloria, whom he had raised himself (being a widower) according to his own hygienic and athletic principles. After we had all bought his booklets, and promised to take up his system of calisthenics, he became quite chummy and showed us a lot of photographs of Gloria at different ages, doing her gymnastic exercises, beginning as a little plump Venus and ending as a stunning profile in tights. We tried to maintain an attitude of merely scientific detachment toward those pictures, admiring them only as connoisseurs of physical culture; but we ended by begging him for copies, insisting that they would be a useful guide to us in our own private exercising. But Larsen said he was keeping them to illustrate a new enlarged edition of his physical-culture book. We told him that it would sell a million copies, and I think we all volunteered to act as selling-agents for the book. Annette Kellermann and Susanna Cocroft, we cried, were scarecrows compared to Gloria.

"To all this banter Gloria would listen calmly and unembarrassed, for she had a magnificent unconsciousness of her own superb allure.

We would each try to get a moment alone with her to describe the exercises we were taking, and to ask her advice about our muscular development. I remember that Blackmore, after secret practice that we had not suspected, took the wind out of our sails one evening when some of us were bragging of our accomplishment in bending and touching the floor while standing on tiptoe. He jumped up and caught hold of the lintel of the doorway, and chinned himself on it a dozen times or so. We were all crestfallen by this feat until Gloria came forward—all the other customers had gone home—and did the same thing about twenty times. She went back to her counter with a heavenly flush of pride, while Blackmore dashed to a table and did a little sketch of her from memory, with the lovely lines of her figure silhouetted against the doorway.

"But it was I who was first to think of the subtlest compliment that any one could pay her, which was to ask the privilege of feeling her biceps. And what an arm she had! Not a great, fleshy, flabby washerwoman's limb, but the rippling marble of a Greek statue brought to warm life! Blackmore used to sit at meal-times neglecting his protose steak and making sketches of her while she wasn't looking. The best I could do was write verses about her. And while she played no favourites, I think she really gave me a little the inside track, because I talked physical culture with her more seriously than the others, who tried to make love to her a little too baldly.

"By this time she had us all doing calisthenics. The creaky floors of Mrs. Vesey's house used to resound night and morning with the agonies of our gymnastics. There was one exercise that Gloria told us she found particularly helpful. It was to lie down with the feet under a bureau or any other heavy piece of furniture, extend the arms behind the head, and then raise and lower the body a hundred times, pivoting from the waist. This was only one of fifty or more laborious accomplishments that we undertook for the sake of our goddess. No woman was ever wooed with more honest pangs, or with more repeated genuflections. As we lay on the floor before going to bed, raising our legs in the air two hundred times, or groaned in some sinew-cracking, twisting contortion devised by the pitiless Swede, it was the vision of Gloria's beauty of snow and rose that gave us courage. If any passer-by ever looked up at the front of Mrs. Vesey's house in the early mornings, he must have been startled to see a white figure near every window, furiously going through the Swedish manual. One of us, we fondly thought, would some day spend a healthy Swedish honeymoon performing these

59

motions in ecstatic company with Gloria; and we did not want to be shamed by her incomparable perfection. If she worshipped bodily symmetry, our goal was nothing less. We wanted to be lithe, supple, very panthers of elasticity and grace. The evening I was able to stand on one leg in the restaurant and proudly raise my other foot to touch a gas-jet some six feet from the floor, I felt that Gloria might some day be mine."

Dove paused again, and seemed to fall into a reminiscent reverie. Unconsciously he stiffly extended one leg in front of him, and I divined that he was inwardly rehearsing that act of calisthenic triumph.

"By gracious!" he said, "I've never forgotten the night I got her father's permission to take her to some gymnastic tournament, or something of that sort, down at Madison Square Garden. How annoyed the other men were when they went to the chop-house that night for their evening penance of lentils, and found Gloria absent! Yes, it was an odd wooing. I had found the measurements of the Venus de Milo in some Sunday paper, and that night, when we became quite sentimental, I made her promise to take her own dimensions, so that we could compare the proportions of the two. And we had some very happy little jokes, quite simple ones that she would understand, about her arms being much more lovely than those of the statue, and that sort of thing. How deliciously she blushed the next day when she gave me her list of measurements, written out on a sheet of paper. Of course, I pretended not to understand which was which. I wrote a little poem about them."

"It seems to me," I said, "that you were getting on very well. What was the trouble? You didn't marry her, did you?"

"Old man Larsen," he continued, gravely, "had a number of other hobbies besides vegetarianism and physical culture. He was a mechanical genius in his way. I remember once, after we had expressed exaggerated admiration of some atrocious compound of lentils and nuts and fruit, Gloria took us through the kitchen to show us an ingenious sandwich-making machine her father had contrived. You fed in loaves of pumpernickel bread and pats of nut butter on one side, hard-boiled eggs and lettuce and dressing on the other, and out came egg-salad sandwiches through a slot, as neat as you could want to see. But the best of his stunts was a sort of miniature vacuum cleaner which the waitresses used for taking the crumbs off the tables. You've seen those little hot-air pistols they use at swell shoe-shining stands to dry the liquid cleanser off your shoes before they put on the polishing paste? Well, Larsen's decrumbing machine, as we used to call it, looked rather like those. You screwed a plug into an electric light socket, ran the little gun over the table, and in a jiffy it sucked up crumbs and cigarette ashes and spilled lentils and matches, and left the cloth neat. Larsen was so proud of it he said he was going to patent it.

"I never cared so very much for the old man, he was a little too eccentric; and I began to think, after a while, that he used his daughter a little too crudely as a business bait; but he was full of ideas. He had a big motor-truck that he used to cruise around town, visiting the markets himself, to get the pick of the vegetables; and he was always tinkering with that truck, planning new mechanical tricks of some kind. He had an insatiable curiosity, too. He used to sit down at the table with us sometimes, late in the evening, and ask about our work, and where we lived, and what Mrs. Vesey was like, and what time of day we were home, and all sorts of fool questions like that.

"Well, the time went on, and it began to be cold weather. I noticed this sooner than the other fellows, I think, because whereas most of them went to offices during the daytime, I stayed home at Mrs. Vesey's, trying to write in my narrow coop of a top bedroom. You know how depressing an instrument a typewriter is when your hands are cold. I haven't forgotten some dreary vigils I had up there, struggling to write short stories. Sometimes I used to give it up weakly, and go round to Larsen's, where it was always warm and cozy, to drink herb coffee and eat those brittle Swedish biscuits and chat with Gloria. I used to complain to her about the cold in my room, and she would laugh and say that I just ought to try a winter in Sweden.

"'Swedish exercises,' she would say. 'That's the thing to stir up your blood! They'll keep you warm.'

"And then, in her enchanting way, she would tell me a new one, and if there were no customers (as there generally weren't in the middle of the afternoon) she would illustrate how it should be done. Sometimes she would even allow me what she called a Swedish kiss—a very fleeting and provocative embrace. And then I would show her my new perfection in doing the backward stoop or some such muscular oddity, and return to my cold citadel.

"But in spite of the fact that we were all busy much of the time going through our manual of exercises, presently the chill of Mrs. Vesey's

61

lodgings became severe. Mrs. Vesey was a rather obstinate and frugal old dear, and she herself dwelt down in the kitchen, where her big gas-range kept her comfortable. When we complained of the cold, she had all sorts of excuses for postponing lighting the furnace. There was a big coal strike that year, and she was quite right in suspecting that once her present supply was exhausted it would be very hard to get more. Also, she said, her furnace man had quit, but she was hunting for another. On one pretext or another, she kept on putting us off, until finally it was mid-November, and we were doing our exercises in rooms where our breath showed like clouds of fog. And then one day Mrs. Vesey came up in great glee to say that a coal man had called that very morning, of his own accord, and had offered to give her five tons. She had promptly snapped at the chance, and he had put the coal in the cellar; so we should have heat the very next day, when the new furnace man was expected.

"Naturally we were all cheered by this good news. We sped round to Larsen's restaurant in high spirits, and adored our divinity with even more than usual abandon.

"'Now my fingers will be warm again, Gloria,' I said, 'I'll be able to write some more poems about you.'

"'Yes,' cried Blackmore, 'and now it will be warm enough for you to come and pose for me in my lovely attic at Mrs. Vesey's. If you had come before, I should have called my painting "The Chilblain Venus."'

"'Silly boys!' said Gloria, with that delicious, soft Swedish accent which I can't even try to imitate. 'You are hot-blooded enough as it is. You don't need all that warming up. Look at us vegetarians; you make fun of us, but our lentils keep our blood circulating. Try Brussels sprouts; they are full of calories.'

"'Ah!' we shouted. 'But you seem to keep this place warm enough.'

"Old Larsen, who passed through the room just then, broke in crossly:

"'We have to, for the sake of the customers,' he said. 'Gloria, stop fooling with the gentlemen and attend to business.' He seemed in a bad humour that night.

"The next day must have been some sort of holiday, for I know we all went out to see a football game. We got back about supper-time

62

and found the house perishing chill. With shouts and protests we called Mrs. Vesey from her kitchen, but she explained that the expected furnace man had not turned up.

"'Well,' said Blackmore, 'this can't go on any longer, Mrs. Vesey. I'll go down and light the fire myself. We'll take turns and keep it going till your man comes.'

"He ran down to the basement, but a minute later he was up again.

"'Mrs. Vesey,' he shouted, 'what is all this nonsense? Are you kidding us? There's no coal down there at all!'

"'No coal?' she exclaimed. 'Why, there was a good three or four tons, and the man said he put five tons more in yesterday. I heard him do it—never heard such a noise in my life. I paid him ten dollars a ton.'

"'Impossible!' Blackmore cried, angrily. 'There's not enough down there to fry Nemo with. About three shovelfuls, that's all. What is this—some kind of a game to freeze us out?'

"Mrs. Vesey wrung her hands, and we all ran down to the cellar. It was as Blackmore had said. The bins were empty, save for a few lumps."

Dove gazed down thoughtfully at the coal office on the pier below us, where a wagon was loading.

"On a mellow afternoon like this," he said, "coal doesn't seem quite so pressing a concern; but I tell you, in a bleak boarding-house about Thanksgiving time, with no heat of any sort available but a gas-jet, it is a different matter. We were an angry and puzzled lot that night. Mrs. Vesey protested so pitifully that there had been coal in the bins only the day before, and asserted so repeatedly that she had heard the noise of the new load going in, that we could not help believe her. She promised to call up her coal man the first thing the next morning, and we also agreed to go round and visit him in a body, to add our personal appeals; but how on earth several tons of coal could have been stolen out of the cellar without any one hearing it seemed to us a mystery.

"The next morning we visited the coal-dealer en masse—in a coalition, as Blackmore said—and by spirited imprecation and paying cash we extracted a promise to have a couple of tons sent at once. His office was some distance up on Columbus Avenue, and on our way back we passed through one of the cross-streets—Eighty-Third, I think it was, because one of us wanted to get some stamps at the post-office. As we came along, we heard the rumble of coal passing down a chute, and saw a coal-wagon in the distance.

"'There's somebody in luck,' said one.

"'But what an odd-looking coal-wagon,' said another, as we approached.

"It was a large motor-truck with a hinged metal top, something like a huge street-cleaning cart. The engine was throbbing, and the coal was roaring noisily in the chute, which led down into the cellar window of a brownstone dwelling. The chute, instead of being the customary shallow trough, was a large circular pipe, so that we could not actually see the coal pouring downward, but only hear it crashing through the metal tube. That struck me as a good idea for preventing the coal-dust from spreading over everything near.

"But we were all interested not only in the odd appearance of the truck, but in the extraordinary din it caused. Delivering coal is never a silent job, naturally; but this racket was really terrific. The driver seemed to have left his engine running full tilt, and the whole truck quivered and shook with the power. We stood amazed at the furious rattle and uproar. The noise was too great for spoken words to be caught, but I pointed out the circular chute to Blackmore. It was made in telescoping sections, to slide into itself, and was an interesting novelty.

"It occurred to me that this dealer, whoever he might be—there was no name on the truck—could perhaps let Mrs. Vesey have some coal. We could see the feet of the driver, who was standing on the other side of the truck, and I went round to speak to him. It was a stocky man with a flowing bush of black beard and wearing a suit of very grimy overalls. At the top of my voice I yelled:

"'Got any coal to sell?'

"He shook his head in a surly way and turned his back on me.

"I could not tell from his gesture whether he had answered my question, or was indicating that he could not hear; so I shouted at him again.

"At the same time I noticed Blackmore and the others gathered at

64

the cellar window, looking in curiously over the slope of the delivery pipe. The coal man seized a lever and shut off his power, for the engine stopped, and after a little sliding and rumbling in the tube the racket ceased. He picked up a shovel and ran to the group by the chute.

"'Here, let that alone!' he cried, angrily. "'Keep your shirt on,' said Blackmore. 'We're just looking at this outfit of yours. It makes a devil of a noise. Regular public nuisance, I call it!' "'It's none of your affair,' said the man. 'Keep out of what don't concern you.'

"He returned to his truck, pulled a handle, and the roar of the coal began again. I was standing near him, while the others were on the opposite side of the wagon, so I was the only one to see a curious thing. There were several revolving cogwheels at the side of the truck, and in his irritation, I suppose the driver stooped over them too closely. At any rate, his beard caught in the cogs, and I gave a cry of dismay, thinking he would be cruelly hurt. To my amazement the beard was whisked quickly from his face, and I saw that he was Larsen. He looked at me with an expression of alarm and anger that was laughable.

"'When did you turn coal-dealer?' I shouted. But at this moment Blackmore, who was still bending over the chute, sprang up and ran round to us. He, too, was staggered to see the identity of the driver. He dragged me a few paces away and shouted in my ear.

"'Damn queer business,' he said. 'That coal isn't going in. It's coming out!'

"'What the deuce do you mean?' I said.

"'Just what I say. He's got some sort of a suction engine in that truck, a kind of big vacuum cleaner, and he's simply siphoning the coal out of somebody's cellar.'

"Larsen ran at us with a big spanner in his hand, but we grappled with him, and while three of us held him the others examined the truck. It was perfectly true. By an ingenious gasoline pump installed in the wagon he was drawing out the coal. Looking into the top of the wagon through a little glass peephole, we could see the black nuggets coming swiftly up out of the chute. By this time a little crowd had gathered, and the lady of the house ran out to see what was happening. I think she thought we were trying to seduce her coal supply. She explained angrily to us that Larsen had driven up to

65

her door half an hour before and offered to sell her several tons of coal. Her cellar, like everyone else's, was none too well stocked, and she had been delighted to agree.

"While we were wondering just what to do, Larsen, who had been glaring wickedly at us, broke away from our grasp and reversed his machinery so that the coal began to thunder back honestly into the cellar. The puzzled woman, not suspecting anything wrong, went back indoors after we made some impromptu explanation for the fuss. Larsen's amputated black beard whirled round and round, still adhering to the rolling cogs, as we watched, while he stood by sullenly. We walked away down the block to hold a council, and also to let the group of mystified onlookers disperse. Of course, our first thought was to go for the police; but then we thought of Gloria."

Dove sighed, and tapped out his long-expired pipe.

"Well," he said, "that's pretty near the end of the story. I'm afraid association with Beauty blunts the sense of rectitude. No, we didn't do anything about it, except see to it that Larsen put back that coal in the cellar. I suppose we were really accessory to a misdemeanour, because we gathered from some small paragraphs we saw in the papers that a number of householders in that neighbourhood had been mysteriously robbed of their coal. To tell you the truth, we couldn't bear the thought of taking any action that would ruin Gloria's happiness. What were a few tons of black, filthy coal compared to that serene and golden-white beauty of hers, like some princess in a Norse fairy tale? The old man was a lunatic, we supposed, and would come to grief sooner or later. We were not going to be the ones to bring humiliation upon him.

"We walked back, stricken, to our lodgings; and as we passed the Physical Culture Chophouse we looked furtively through the window. We could see Gloria laying the tables for lunch, the tall, strong curve of her back as she leaned over, her capable white hands smoothing the cloth. None of us had the heart to go in.

"We clubbed together to pay for Mrs. Vesey's new supply of coal, although it broke our pocket-books for the next month or so. We were too hard up, then, to go on eating at Larsen's. We had to patronize a lunch-counter instead, where we gloomed over frankfurters and beans and quarrelled with one another, in sheer misery, as to which one of us Gloria had really liked best. We never saw her again, because about a week later the Larsen café shut up, and they disappeared."

66

"And the calisthenics?" I said. "Did you go on with those?"

"No," he said; "we were too melancholy. Also, as soon as Mrs. Vesey's coal arrived, we didn't need to. That was the terrible part of it. You see, Gloria had simply egged us on to do those exercises so that we wouldn't feel the chill when her father stole the coal. I'm afraid she was as guilty as he was, but we tried to convince ourselves that she was only a tool."

We got up from our bench, for the afternoon air was growing bleak.

"Now you know," he said, "why that coal-dump down there reminded me of Gloria. Well, it was wonderful while it lasted—until, as you might say, the serpent drove us out of our Garden of Sweden."

THE COMMUTATION CHOPHOUSE

IT WAS two days before Christmas, and Dove Dulcet had come down town to have lunch with me. As he had arrived rather early, we were taking a little stroll round the bright, windy streets before our meal, enjoying the colour and movement of the scene. We stopped by St. Paul's churchyard to note the curious contrast of the old chocolate spire relieved against the huge glittering shaft of the Woolworth Building. At the noon hour St. Paul's stands in the dark shadow of the great cliffs to the south, while the Woolworth pinnacle leaps up like a spearhead into the golden vacancy of day-long sunshine.

"Saint Paul in the shadow, Saint Frank in the sun," said Dove with gentle irony. "It seems to prove that ten cents put in the cash register gets nearer Heaven than ten cents dropped in the collection plate."

When Dove is philosophical, he is always full of quaint matter, but I was hardly heeding what he said. My eye had been caught by a crowd gathered at the corner of Church Street. Over the heads of the throng was a winking spark of light that flashed this way and that as though spun from a turning mirror.

"Let's go and see what's doing," I said. My poet friend is always docile, and he followed me down Fulton Street.

"It looks to me like a silk hat," he said.

And so it was. On the corner of the pavement stood a tall, stout, and very well-nourished man with a ruddy face, wearing shabby but still presentable cutaway coat and gray trousers, and crowned by a steep and glittering stovepipe hat which twinkled like a heliograph in the dazzling winter glare. But, most amazing, when we elbowed a passage through the jocular crowd, we saw that this personable individual was wearing, instead of an overcoat, two large sandwich boards vigorously lettered as follows:

THE COMMUTATION CHOPHOUSE

OPENS TO-DAY 59 Ann Street
Celebrate the Merry Yuletide!
One Prodigious Meal,

$1 BUY A STRIP TICKET AND SAVE MONEY

TO-DAY ONLY 100 meals for $10

This corpulent sandwich man was blithely answering the banter of those who were not awed by the radiance of his headgear and the dignity of his mien, and passing out printed cards to those nearest him.

"Do all the hundred meals have to be eaten to-day?" asked Dulcet. "If so, the task is beyond my powers."

"Like the man in the Bible," I said, "he probably rented his garments. But he couldn't rent that admirable abdomen that proclaims him a well-fed man. It seems to me a very sound ad. for the chophouse."

"Unquestionably," said my friend, gravely, "he is the man who put the ad in adipose."

The sandwich man, unabashed by these remarks, handed me one of his cards, which Dulcet and I read together:

K. Jefferson Gastric, the best-fed man south of 42nd Street, takes this importunity of urging you to become a steakholder in the Commutation Chophouse. Why pay for overhead expense? In the Commutation Chophouse all unnecessaries are discarded and you pay only for food, not for finger-bowls and a lovely female cashier. No tips. To-day Only, the Opening Day, to celebrate the jovial Yule, the management will sell Strip Tickets entitling you to 100 Glorious Meals, for $10.

At this point a policeman politely urged Mr. Gastric to move on, and he passed genially down Church Street, his resplendent hat glowing above a trail of followers.

"Come on," I said; "it's time to eat, anyway. Let's go over to Ann Street and have a look at this philanthropic venture."

"Well," said Dulcet, "since it's your turn to buy, far be it from me to protest."

The narrow channel of Ann Street is always crowded at the lunch hour, but on that occasion it was doubly congested with patrons of the amusing toyshops. We pushed patiently along, and passing

Nassau Street moved into a darker and shabbier region. A sound of music rose upon the air. To our surprise, at the entrance to an unsuspected alley stood a fiddler playing a merry jig. Beside him was another sandwich man, also stout and well-favoured and in Fifth-Avenue attire, carrying boards which read:

ENTRANCE TO THE COMMUTATION CHOPHOUSE

Eat Drink and Be Merry For To-morrow We Die

To-day Only, for the Jocund Yule,

Strip Tickets for 100 Square Meals, $10

"This is highly diverting," I said. "Apparently we go down this passage. Come on, everyone seems bound the same way. We won't get a seat unless we make haste."

Dulcet was gazing reflectively at the sandwich boards. His blue eyes had a quizzical twinkle.

"For God, for country, and for Yule," he said. "Queer that this should happen on Ann Street. I seem to remember——"

"Queer that it should happen anywhere," I interrupted him. "It's a clever advertising stunt, anyway—100 meals for $10. It seems too good to be true."

"The only thing I'm afraid of," he said, "is that it is literally true."

"Walk in, gents, give us a try," cried the sandwich man. "Try anything once, gents."

"Come on, Dove," I said, seeing that others were crowding ahead of us down the alley. "None of your paradoxes!"

The narrow passage turned into a courtyard overlooked by old grimy warehouses with iron-shuttered windows. In one corner was a fine substantial brick building with a rounded front, and a long flight of wooden stairs that seemed to lead up to a marine junk shop, for old sea-boots and ships' lanterns and fenders hung along the wall. In a basement was an iron foundry where we could see the bright glow of a forge. Halfway down the little area was a low door with a huge stone lintel-piece over which was a large canvas sign: the commutation chophouse.

70

I must confess to an irrational affection for quaint eating places, and having explored downtown New York's crowded cafés and lunchrooms rather carefully in quest of a congenial tavern, the Commutation Chophouse struck me as highly original and pleasing. We stepped down into a very large and rather dark cellar that apparently had previously been used as a carpenter's shop, for a good many traces of the earlier tenancy were still visible. The furnishings were of the plainest, consisting simply of heavy wooden tables and benches. There was no linen on the tables, but the wood had been scrubbed scrupulously clean and there were piles of tissue napkins. From a door at the back waiters came rushing with trays of food. A glorious clatter of knives and forks filled the air, and it looked at first as though we would find no place to sit. As Dove expressed it, the room was loaded to the muzzle; and a continuous stream of patrons was coming down the alley, allured by the sandwich man and the absurd thin gayety of the fiddle. By the front door stood a dark young man, behind a small counter, selling tickets.

"One meal for a dollar," he cried, repeatedly, as he took in money. "One hundred meals for ten dollars. Get your commutation tickets here."

"We'll try two single meals to begin with," I said, and put down a ten-dollar bill.

The young man rummaged in a drawer full of greasy notes to get the change. "Better get a commutation," he said. "Tremendous saving."

"I should think you'd need a cash register," said Dulcet. "Handling all that kale, it would be useful in keeping the accounts straight."

The young man looked up sharply.

"Say," he retorted, "what are you, mister? Cash-register salesman? Step along please, don't block the gangway. Next! Seats in the rear! No, commutation tickets not transferable. Good only to the purchaser. Ten dollars, please. Next!"

"They seem to be coining money," said Dove, as we found places at last in a rear corner.

"Well," I said, "this is just the kind of place I like. By Jove, this building must be well over a hundred years old. Look at those beams in the ceiling. All they need is a few sporting prints and an

71

open fireplace. Lit by candles, too, you see. Well, well, this is the real alehouse atmosphere. Why, it's as good as the Cheshire Cheese. This is the kind of place where I can imagine Doctor Johnson and Charles Lamb sitting in a corner."

"You are an incurable sentimentalist," he said. "Besides, Lamb would have had to sit on Johnson's knee, I expect. If I remember rightly, Lamb was a very small urchin when Doctor Johnson died."

"Why be so literal?" I protested. "Haven't you any sentiment for fine antique flavour, and all that sort of thing?"

"If there is one thing where sentiment plays no part with me," he said, "it is food. At meal times I am distinctly a realist. Fine antique flavour is rather upsetting when you find it in your meat. But still," he continued, "I must admit this looks good." He beamed approvingly at the thick chop and baked potatoes and beans and coffee the waiter had put down in front of us.

"Evidently you don't order your food," I said. "They give you the standardized meal of the day. Fall to! These beans baked in cheese strike me as excellent."

I have never seen waiters rush around with such speed as they did in that crowded cellar, where flickering candle-gleams cast a tawny light over the crowded tables of men packed shoulder to shoulder. They flashed in and out through the rear door like men possessed. They careered in with trays of steaming viands, crashed them down on the bare tables, and fled out again, napkins streaming behind them like pennants. Once they had delivered your food it seemed impossible to catch their gaze, for we tried to hail one to ask for ketchup. It was no use. He flew hither and yon with frantic and single-minded energy.

"These waiters speed like dervishes," I said. "Evidently the no-tip rule does not lessen their zeal."

"Perhaps they get a share in the profits of the enterprise," said Dulcet, placidly.

Just behind us was a small barred window looking out on a street. It was at the ground level, and looking through the dusty pane I could see horses' hoofs going by, and the feet of pedestrians. Suddenly there was a great clang and crash outside, and I turned to look.

"What's up?" said Dulcet, who was cheerfully disposing of his chop as well as his neighbour's elbow would permit him.

"They seem to have spilled some beans," I said, peering through the dusky aperture. "There's a truck delivering food or something at the back door. They've tipped over a can, I think."

"Spilled some beans?" he said, with his first sign of real interest. "That sounds symbolic. Let me have a look."

He stood up on the bench and gazed outward. Presently he sat down again and went on calmly with his meal. Some excellent cheese cake was brought us as dessert.

"That alley behind us," he said. "I suppose it communicates with Beekman Street, doesn't it?"

"I guess so. Why?"

"Just wondering. Ben, I apologize for my skepticism. The food here is jolly good. In fact, it's so good that I think I've tasted it before. I am your debtor for a very enlarging experience. And now, as the crowd is becoming almost oppressive, and I can see that there are others eager to commute, suppose we smoke our cigars outdoors."

"Right you are," I said. "And since the food is eatable, and I happen to have the money with me, I think I'll invest in one of those strip tickets. Everyone else seems to be doing it, and it looks to me a good way to save money. A hundred lunches—why, that will see me through till spring. I don't think I'll get tired of eating here, it's so amusing."

"No," said Dove, as he picked up his hat, "I don't think you'll get tired of eating here. Perhaps the money will be well spent."

I bought my commutation, and we stood in the shabby old courtyard for a few minutes watching the crowd stream in. A good many, I noticed, though unable to find seats, still took advantage of the opening-day offer and bought the hundred meal tickets for future consumption.

"The only drawback about this place is the crowd," I said. "If this keeps up, half of downtown New York will be eating here."

"Look here," said Dove, "I think I shall be down this way again to-morrow. It's my turn to buy. Will you lunch with me then? We'll celebrate the jovial Yule together."

73

"Fine," I said. "Meet you at the old red newspaper-box at the corner of Broadway and Vesey to-morrow at 12 o'clock."

We were both there punctually.

"Have you got your appetite with you?" asked Dove. "It's a bit early for feasting, but it'll give us time for a stroll after lunch."

"Where do we eat?" I said. "Commutation again? It's all velvet to me, anyway, all my lunches are paid for for the next three months."

"There's a little place on Beekman Street I used to know," he said. "Let's try that."

We found a corner table in an odd old eating house at the corner of Beekman and Gold streets, which I had never seen before.

"I'm a great believer in tit for tat, fair play, and all that sort of thing," said Dulcet when the waiter approached. "You gave me an excellent lunch yesterday. I intend to give you the same lunch to-day, if you can stand eating it again. Waiter! Mutton chop, baked potato, baked beans, coffee, and cheese cake. For two."

When the beans came, baked with cheese in a little brown dish, just as they were served the day before, I must confess that I was startled.

"Why, these beans are done exactly like those we had at the Commutation," I said. "Are these people doing the cooking for the chop-house?"

"Perhaps you'll have to eat chop and beans for a hundred lunches," Dulcet said. "Well, it's a hearty diet. After all, the sandwich boards simply said a hundred meals. They didn't guarantee that they would be different."

I insisted that on our way back toward the office we should stop at the Commutation Chophouse and find out from a customer what the bill of fare had been on the second day. The vision of a hundred repetitions of any meal, however good, is rather ghastly.

"I don't hear the minstrel to-day," Dove observed as we drew near the alley.

"Oh, well," I said, "that was just to draw business for the opening."

We turned down the passage at No. 59. Quite a crowd of patrons were waiting their turn, I saw. They were standing in the courtyard by the chop-house door, talking busily.

"You see," I said, "it's still crowded."

We reached the entrance. The door was closed. The sign over the doorway now had additional lettering painted on it, and read:

THE COMMUTATION CHOPHOUSE

The Other 99 Meals Will Be Served In Augusta, Maine.

"Come on, Ben," said Dulcet. "No use trying to break through a window. There's no one there. I wonder what the fare is to Augusta?"

"You rascal!" I cried. "If you suspected this, why the devil did you encourage me to squander my $10?"

"I simply said it would probably be well spent," he said, with a clear blue humorous gaze. "If it helps to cauterize your magnificent credulity, it will be."

We sat down on a bench in St. Paul's churchyard to smoke a pipe together while I performed some mental obsequies over my vanished Federal Reserve certificate. Dove looked up at the sparkling gilded turret of the Woolworth.

"I daresay Frank Woolworth would have fallen for it, too," Dove said. "The idea of a hundred meals for 10 cents each would have appealed to him. But you know, old man, there are certain fixed and immutable laws that the observant city dweller is accustomed to. My motto is, whenever you find an apparent exception to those laws, look for an enigma in the woodpile. I suspected something wrong when I saw that sandwich man on Church Street. A man as fat as that doesn't generally take a job sandwiching. Also I have doubts about people who insist on calling Christmas 'Yule'. Moreover, a man doesn't generally take a job sandwiching until his shirt is so ragged that he is ashamed to exhibit it in public, when he is glad to cover it up with the boards. Those two fat sandwicheers were members of the firm, I fear, for their linen was O. K. And, secondly, what are the first things a man gets if he really intends to start a restaurant? A cash register and a bunch of ketchup bottles.

There wasn't a cash register nor a ketchup bottle in sight in the Commutation Chophouse. No, my dear; what you admired as carefully arranged atmosphere of antiquity, the plain board tables and candles and so on, was really stark cheapness. They weren't spending any money on overhead; they said so themselves.

"When you called my attention to the spilled beans, I was sure. For they were not merely beans: they were baked beans; a far more significant matter. When I looked out of the window I could see at once that there was no kitchen attached to the Commutation Chophouse. The food was all being delivered from that place on Beekman Street, whose name was on the truck. A few ingenious rogues simply rented that old cellar, cheaply enough I guess, put in a few tables, arranged to have grub shipped in from near by, printed their commutation tickets, and sat down to collect as many dollars as they could lure out of the open-handed Christmas throng."

"Well, of all infernal liars," I cried, "they certainly take the prize."

"Not so," said Dulcet as we got up to go. "You should have read the sandwich boards a little more carefully. Their ingenious author, whom you chide as the Ann Street Ananias, really told the exact and circumstantial truth."

We stood at the gateway of the graveyard, and gazed across the roaring traffic of Broadway. Dove smiled and said he must be starting on his Christmas shopping.

"I tried to warn you," he said, "but you wouldn't listen. As I was about to say just before we visited the place, it was queer that it should happen on Ann Street. Don't you remember that a certain famous gentleman had his museum at the corner of Broadway and Ann? And it was he, I think, who remarked that there's one born every minute. Well, Merry Christmas!"

THE PERT LITTLE HAT

HEMMING had a home, and dearly he loved everything in it—with one exception. He loved the furnace, and the kitchen range with its warm ruddy glow, and the violet-coloured wafer of expensive aromatic soap that always mysteriously appeared on the marble wash-basin when visitors came. He loved the little glass towel racks, and the miniature embroidered hand towels with Mrs. Hemming's maiden initials on them, which also appeared, white and fragrant, whenever there was any special festivity. Those little towels were to him a kind of symbol of the first ecstatic days of their married life, and he could not bear to think of the inevitable time when they would be frayed and discarded. He loved the shelf over the fireplace where his brown-stained corncob pipe waited for the after-supper smoke. He loved the little porch where the baby carriage stood, and the tulip beds that he and Janet had planted together, and the mission dining table, now blistered and scarred, that had been their very first piece of furniture.

But in the little den upstairs stood his desk, and how he hated it!

Hemming, you see, had literary ambitions, and that desk meant to him every circumstance, every long-drawn torment, of weariness and toil. It had meant much pleasure, too, in hours when his writing had prospered; but how the bitter outnumbered the sweet! How many hundred evenings he had dragged himself to it, in lassitude and lethargy; had forced his drowsy, unwilling mind to the task at hand. How many nights, nodding over the typewriter, he had stumbled on and on. Over his desk he kept, ironically, a letter he had once had from an editor, which said: We like stories. They have a joyous freshness. You write as though you enjoyed it.

Hemming was no quick and easy composer. His stories emerged slowly, painfully, hammered and wrenched from the stubborn tissues of a weary brain. When his whole soul and body cried out for a comfortable stretch on the couch, with pipe and book, and a gradual, blissful lapse into slumber, he would throw off his coat, stick his head out of the window for a dozen gulps of cool night air, and then sit down at the wheezy old typewriter.

Its yellow keys seemed a kind of doleful rosary on which he told long petitions to whatever gods look down pityingly on young writers. He would think how wonderful it would be if he could only do his writing in the morning when he was fresh. To leap out of bed in the crisp early air, to plunge into the cold bath where the water shimmered a pale green by catching the tint of the big maple tree just outside the bathroom, to swallow two cups of hot coffee, two slices of buttered toast, and then sit down to his desk. In the zest and lustihood of the morning, how the thoughts would throng, how the great empire of words would unroll before him, far away to the blue hills where lived his unwritten poems! Such was his daily thought as he hurried down the hill on bright mornings to catch the 8.13 train to town. But to come back at night after a long day at the office, and after helping Janet wash the dishes, and stoking the furnace or mowing the lawn or planting bulbs in the garden—then to try to write seemed tough indeed.

Still, it had to be done, and Hemming threw his manhood into the task. In his little den there was just space for a couch, his desk, and his books, which were littered about the room. His only chance of accomplishing anything was to get Janet safely installed on the couch, for if he once lay down there work was impossible. She would curl up under a steamer rug, tired out from a long day with the house and the baby, reading a book or the evening paper. And then the stumbling clatter of the typewriter would begin.

After a while there always came what they humorously called "the pathetic little moment." This was the time when Janet's book or paper would slip from her hand, she would turn away from the light, and coast down the long, smooth toboggan of sleep. Then Hemming would switch off the reading lamp above her head (with the secret economic satisfaction young householders always feel when they switch off a light), touch the soft cheek with a friendly finger, and climb the keys once more. His writing always seemed to go better after the "pathetic little moment" was past. There was a kind of subconscious satisfaction in the feeling that Janet was there, asleep, and that he was working for her. And Janet used to affirm that there was no lullaby like the irregular thumping of those keys and levers.

There was another catchword they had, which also moved stealthily in the back passages of his mind as he mulled over his manuscripts. Janet badly needed a new bonnet—a "pert little hat," she liked to call it—and Hemming had pledged himself to write something that would bring her the saucy little ornament she craved in time for Christmas. She was a slender, bright-faced creature, and no one could wear an innocently tilted turban with more grace. But these had been hard days for small incomes. Winter coal, and warm clothes for the Urchin, and the cook's wages (when they had one), and Liberty Bonds—all these had taken precedence over the pert little hat. It had been talked of so long, it had become a kind of joyous legend, which Janet hardly expected to see realized on her head. She used to say wistfully, as she coasted off to sleep on the couch: "Would it be unpatriotic to think about the pert little hat?" And her husband would vow that patriotism that excluded pert little hats was no patriotism at all. So he had sworn that the bonnet should be millinered on the clacking loom of his typewriter. They used to laugh about it, and say that the little hat ought to be trimmed with carbon typewriter ribbons.

But Hemming did not know that Janet was not always asleep after the so-called "pathetic moment" when she ostensibly gave up the struggle with drowsiness. The twanging springs of the old couch made less noise than the typewriter keys, but they, too, moved to a secret creative refrain. There were times when Janet lay watching the lamplight on the rows of books, and little pictures of stories that she would like to write flashed into her head. They often used to come to her at inopportune periods during the day, when the Urchin was in his bath or when she was taking stock of the ice-box. Of course her husband was the literary man of the family, and she had no thought of setting up her simple imaginings against his more serious efforts. But one night, when he was engrossed in some intractable plot, Janet slipped away into the little guest room and shut herself in. With a stub pencil, on odd sheets of notepaper, she began scribbling hotly. Two hours later, when Hemming came back to earth and hunted her out, she was still at it.

"What on earth are you up to, monk?" he asked.

"Making out laundry lists," she said.

More observant husbands might have wondered what occasion there would be for a laundry list on Thursday evening, but Hemming was always drowned in his dreams of literary fame.

His story, on which he had laboured at night for two months, and hers, which had taken the spare hours of three days, were finished almost at the same time. After dinner one night, when he had read the manuscript of his story aloud, Janet handed him her venture, with some trepidation. At first he seemed a little nettled that she should have done such a thing.

"Look here, monk," he said, "you oughtn't to wear yourself out

79

trying to write. You have quite enough to do with the house and the baby. Moreover, you don't know how discouraging it is. It takes years of patient apprenticeship before one can get anything across with the editors. This is my job, brownie."

"But I enjoyed doing it," she said.

"That's a bad sign. All really good stories take fearful effort. How long did you spend on this?"

"Oh, quite a while," she said, vaguely. She did not like to admit that her little story had involved no "patient apprenticeship."

He lit his pipe and began reading the sheets on which her quick pencil had flashed with such enthusiasm. She sat with her sewing, watching him shyly.

"Very nice," was his comment; but privately he wondered how he was to avoid hurting her feelings. It seemed to him that the story had all the faults of the amateur.

"Would you submit it anywhere?" she asked, eagerly. "Do you think any magazine would buy it?"

He evaded the question. "Would you like me to type it for you?" he said.

"Oh, would you?"

"I'll tell you what I'll do," he said, "I'll be sending my manuscript to Mr. Edwards to-morrow. I'll type yours and send it, too."

Janet was delighted, and she fell asleep that night with the sweet music of the thumping keys in her ears. As she heard the staccato clicking, she thought: "I wonder how far he has got now? How good of him to take all that trouble to copy my poor little story."

Hemming sat up very late that night, copying Janet's manuscript and planning what to say to Mr. Edwards, the editor of the Colonial Magazine, who had been very cordial to him. He resisted the temptation to alter Janet's naïve phrasing here and there, to improve her technique by recasting some of the situations in her story. It was long past midnight when both manuscripts were ready to go into the stout manila envelope. Then, after some meditation, Hemming added the following note:

I am sending you herewith my new story, and hope you may like it. I am also enclosing a manuscript from my wife. Of course she is an untrained writer—this is her first attempt—but I think her story has a certain charm. Won't you, if you can, give her any encouragement you feel proper? If you would write her a personal note of comment it would mean a great deal to her. You know how tenderly one feels toward one's maiden effort.

Sincerely yours,

Godfrey Hemming.

It was very late when Hemming folded the carefully typed sheets and placed them in the precious envelope. He was utterly weary, which must be the explanation of a curious error he made. It was his custom to type his name and address on a separate sheet of paper which was clipped to the story he was submitting. He put his own name on one sheet, and his wife's on another. But in arranging the manuscripts for the envelope he inadvertently put his name-page with his wife's manuscript, and vice versa. Then he went to bed with the satisfaction of well-earned fatigue, and wondering how soon he would be able to order the "pert little hat".

It was two weeks later, and the Urchin had just murmured himself off into his morning nap, when Janet heard the postman's whistle, and ran down to receive an envelope with the name of the Colonial Magazine engraved upon it. Eagerly she tore it open.

My Dear Mrs. Hemming:

Your husband was good enough to send me the manuscript of your story, which I have read with interest. It is an able piece of work, and shows unusual technical skill for a beginner. But I must caution you not to let your pen follow the track of your husband's method too closely. Naturally enough, perhaps, your style seems to have modeled itself on his: but this is a mistake, because it is quite evident that you have ability enough to strike out on your own line. I wish you would study carefully Mr. Hemming's last story, "Three Is Company," which shows a freshness and spontaneous originality better than anything he has done before. It has a touch of charming humour which is new to his work. If you can do us something of that sort, we shall be only too happy to publish it.

81

I am returning your manuscript with many thanks.

Faithfully yours

Theodore Edwards.

Janet looked at the editor's flowing signature in amazement. "Three Is Company" was her own story. And there, in the Colonial Magazine's envelope, lay the revered pages of Godfrey's masterpiece, returned. The "fresh and spontaneous originality" was hers! A flush of exultation thrilled her: she could almost feel the pert little hat on her head. Instinctively she looked at herself in the mirror over the hall mantelpiece. Was it possible that she was a literary genius, and had never known it?

But then a pang of horror chilled her. What dreadful mistake had happened? Alas, it was only too plain—the two stories had been confused. The editor had thought that her story was Godfrey's. He had read it expecting to find the skill of Godfrey's trained hand. And now how was she to spare her husband the mortification of having his painstaking work rejected, while her prentice sketch had won favour by some fluke? Her loyal heart, entirely devoid of selfish satisfaction, could not bear the thought of this grotesque and unhappy climax for her innocent venture. It was all her fault for meddling with what did not concern her. What business had she to write a better story than Godfrey, anyway? She knew that her husband would be honestly proud of her success and would not grudge her the triumph for an instant, but she felt that the poignance of the situation would be intolerable for her. Much better do without all the pert little hats on Chestnut Street than win one at the expense of Godfrey's feelings.

How could she prevent the bad tidings from reaching him? Even now it might be too late. She flew to the telephone, and with pricking pulses asked for the office of the Colonial. One nervous hand unconsciously flew to her hair, as though she were about to enter the august sanctum of the editor.

"Is this Mr. Edwards?

"Oh, Mr. Edwards, this is Mrs. Hemming, Mrs. Godfrey Hemming, the wife of one of your authors——

"Why, there's been a terrible mistake about our manuscripts, Mr. Edwards, the stories that Mr. Hemming sent you. I've just had your letter, and that story you sent back wasn't mine at all, it was Godfrey's——

"I don't see how you can have made the mistake—

"Yes, the story called 'Three Is Company' is mine, I wrote it, but really it can't possibly be better than the other one because I wrote it in such a hurry, it's my first attempt——

"You want to publish it? But, Mr. Edwards, you simply mustn't, because——

"I can't explain over the telephone. I know you only like it because you thought——

"Will you promise not to do anything about it, and not to tell Mr. Hemming anything, until you get a letter from me?

"You will promise? Oh, thank you so much! I'll write at once.

"Good-bye!"

She hurried to the little white enamelled desk, the same desk where the ill-starred "Three Is Company" had been written.

"This will cure me of trying to write," she thought; "why, I never heard of such a thing—to have one's first story accepted! Mr. Edwards must be mad."

Luckily there was one sheet of her engraved stationery left—the paper that Godfrey had given her, she thought remorsefully. All about her were evidences of his loving care, and she had repaid him by undermining his prestige with the one editor who had been nice to him. A fine way for an author's wife to behave! She seized her pen and wrote:

Dear Mr. Edwards:

As I just told you over the phone, there has been some horrible mistake. How it happened I can't guess. The manuscript you sent back to me is Mr. Hemming's story. The one you say you like and want me to study as a model is my own story, "Three Is Company". I'm sorry you like it, I mean I'm sorry you think it is better than Mr. Hemming's story, which can't be so as it is the first story I ever tried to write. I have decided to withdraw it, I don't want it published, so please send it back to me instantly, and write me a letter saying how amateurish it is. I am sending Mr. Hemming's story back to you, so that now you know who wrote it you can reconsider it. Of course, if you thought it was by me, you naturally considered it as the work of a beginner, and only a poor imitation of Mr. Hemming's style.

I don't want you ever to tell Mr. Hemming that I have written this letter. Just tell him you sent my story back to me because it was not good enough.

Sincerely yours,

Janet Colton Hemming.

The importance Janet attached to this letter may be judged from the fact that she left the baby alone in the house, asleep, while she hurried down to the post-office to mail it, together with Godfrey's manuscript, back to Mr. Edwards. And not even the sympathetic Mr. Edwards ever guessed that on the first page, where Godfrey's careful typing ran in neat lines, she had printed a good luck kiss.

The editor was an honourable man, and though he chuckled a little over Janet's breathless letter he really meant to keep the innocent secret. We hope that no young wives will be lured to destruction by our telling the truth, which was simply this, that Janet's little story was much better than Godfrey's. It might not have happened again in a lifetime, but the enthusiasm of her girlish zeal had carried her pen into a very pretty and moving tale, which the Colonial would have been glad to print. But since she wanted it back, there was nothing for Mr. Edwards to do but comply. Then, that very morning, while he was dictating a note of polite refusal to accompany "Three Is Company" back to the suburbs, who should call at the office but Godfrey, to know what the editor thought of the two stories. The coincidence was too much for Edwards, and thinking that it could do no harm to let Hemming know of his wife's devotion—for young husbands are too likely to be selfish—he told him the whole incident. And Godfrey, with a faint sensation of burning under his eyelids, related the dream of a new bonnet that had inspired "Three Is Company".

"Well, now, look here," said Edwards, "I'm not so awfully keen on this story of yours. It isn't anywhere near up to what you can do—or rather, up to what Mrs. Hemming can do," he added, chuckling. "But you go home and write me a yarn about the pert little hat, and I'll put it in the January number. It'll come out just before Christmas, and I hope you'll get that wife of yours the best bonnet in town on the proceeds. If all writers had wives like yours, perhaps the magazines would make better reading. But for heaven's sake don't tell Mrs. Hemming I gave her away. Wait until she sees the story in the magazine, it'll be a Christmas surprise for her."

On the Saturday before Christmas Hemming took Janet to the city to solemnize the purchase of the pert little hat. Any one who happened to see her wearing it down Chestnut Street that bright winter afternoon knew that the elated pink in her cheek was not all reflected from the red bow on the bonnet's neat brim. As they sat down for a matinée and Janet removed the precious creation, giving it to Godfrey to hold for a moment, he said admiringly:

"Well, the old typing bus isn't such a bad milliner after all, hey, monk?"

And Janet, who would then have denied that such a story as "Three Is Company" ever existed, replied innocently:

"I'm so glad Mr. Edwards turned down my story, grump. I like the pert little hat ever so much better because it came all from you."

Even if the pert little hat should live to be a great-great-grandbonnet, none of its descendants will ever give Janet such pleasure.

URN BURIAL

NEVER quarrel at breakfast is the first maxim for commuters and their wives. Partings in anger mean day-long misery for both, and generally involve telephone calls later in the day, and a box of chocolate-coated maraschino cherries carried home on the 5.18. Marriage (say the philosophers) is a subdivision of the penal code, dedicated to the proposition that men and women are created equal. But the studious observer of matrimonial feints and skirmishes sees very little to verify that daring surmise.

Harry Bennett sipped his breakfast coffee grimly. Its savour had departed: for ninety seconds earlier Mrs. Bennett had fled upstairs in a flush of anger and tears. In five minutes he would have to run for the train; and what man can soothe an outraged wife in five minutes? He ate his toast without relish, gazing sourly on the blue-and-white imitation Copenhagen china, the pretty little porcelain marmalade pot, and the big silver coffee-urn.

The desperate inequality of married life pierced his heart. Why should he have to accept in silence tart remarks uttered by his wife, while the least savagery of his own was cause for tears?

He rushed upstairs to say a few consoling words. The bedroom door was locked. Compassion fled, and he growled furiously through the panels. Then he ran hotly for the train.

It seems unreasonable: but the lives of human beings are not guided by reason. Harry had come to the conclusion that the silver coffee-urn was at the bottom of all their squabbles.

Before Elaine Addison surrendered herself into his capable hands, there had been a competitor for the honour of surrounding her with sectional bookcases, linen closets, potted hydrangeas, and the other authentic trappings of a home.

Aubrey Andrews was the rival warrior. He was the kind of man who always has a lot of crisp greenbacks in a neat leather bill-fold. Harry's hard-earned frogskins were always crumpled in a trousers pocket This may seem trivial, but it distinguishes two totally different classes of men. Aubrey was tall, dark, well groomed; he played billiards and belonged to expensive clubs. It was supposed that his wife would be beyond the reach of financial worries. He kept a horse and easy office hours.

Harry—well, Harry was no aristocrat. He worked hard for what he got, and didn't get much. He was neither tall, nor dark, nor well groomed. But he was a fine, lovable, high-minded chap, and to everyone's surprise, including his own, he got Elaine.

Tennyson had a good deal to do with it, I think. Harry still read Tennyson, although that excellent poet is no longer fashionable, and kept on repeating what Tennyson said about Elaine. And finally Elaine could not help saying, "My Lancelot!" and melting into his arms.

Aubrey gave them a magnificent silver coffee-urn for a wedding present, and presently enlisted for service, first on the Mexican border and then in France, where he became a heroic and legendary figure, surrounded in Elaine's mind by the prismatic glamour of girlhood days.

That coffee-urn was a stunner! It was far the handsomest thing in the little suburban house, except, of course, Elaine herself. Beneath its shining caldron sat an alcohol lamp that rendered a blue flame and kept the coffee hot. Elaine's initials—her maiden initials—were engraved upon it, and those of the donor: E. A. A. A. The hand of the insidious silversmith had twined the A's together very gracefully.

Every time he looked at it, Harry felt subconsciously irritated, although he hardly realized why.

It stood on the little mission sideboard, outshining everything else in the pretty dining room. It was Elaine's particular pride, and was used only on special occasions. Often it was brought out for the little celebrations that young married couples have every now and then. And, curiously enough, these celebrations very often ended in tears. The polished dazzle of those silver curves was only too apt to suggest to Elaine's radiant little beauty-loving heart other handsome wares she would like to have, or unlucky comparison of the relative beauty of the wedding presents sent by her friends and his; or Harry would make some blunt remark about his not being able to give her all that some other husband might have.

Alas! Something of the sardonic spirit of the black-browed Aubrey seemed to radiate from his urn. Can a coffee-um hypnotize?

Grotesque as it appears, little by little they realized that the innocent piece of silver was marring many an otherwise happy hour.

All the way to town in the smoking car, Harry's mind rotated savagely about their absurd tiff.

Let's see, how was it? He had said: "I'm sorry, dearest; I shall have to be rather late tonight. The head of my department is away, and I've got an extra lot of work to do." She said: "Oh, dear—oh, dear! Then we sha'n't be able to go to the theatre, shall we?" He said: "We can go next week, Brownie." She said: "Something horrid always happens when we have this coffee-urn on the table."

(N. B. Right here, when the danger topic was introduced, he should have put on an extra soft pedal. But did he? Not a bit. As soon as the urn was mentioned his eyes began to flash.)

"Well," he said, "don't let's have it on so often!" She said: "Any one might think you were jealous of it. It's the only handsome piece of silver I've got."

Here he did make one honest effort to steer away from danger:

"I'm awfully sorry about to-night, honey, but the work's just got to be done." She said: "Why didn't you let me know sooner you were going to work late? I could have arranged to go and see Mother." He said: "Oh, well, everything I do is always wrong, anyway! I suppose if I could buy you a roomful of silver like that old tureen, you wouldn't mind."

And after that it was not far to the deluge. All conducted according to the recognized technique of quarrelling, passing through the seven stages of repartee outlined by Touchstone, which should never be forgotten by those happily married:

> 1 The retort courteous
> 2 The quip modest
> 3 The reply churlish
> 4 The reproof valiant
> 5 The counter-check quarrelsome
> 6 The lie with circumstance
> 7 The lie direct

All day both Mr. and Mrs. Bennett were unpleasantly conscious of their undigested altercation lying black and gloomy in the back of their minds. At lunch-time he tried to call her on the telephone; but the wire did not answer. Indeed, she had gone to spend the day in town with friends, and was to go to dinner and the theatre with them. She left no message for Harry, and gave the cook permission to go out overnight.

About nine o'clock he got home tired and eager to resume their usual blissful companionship. The house was dark and untenanted. In a rage, he threw away the box of candy he had brought, and got himself some bread and cheese from the ice-box.

In the dining room his eye fell upon the coffee-urn. He swore at it. Just then Elaine called him up, and in a cool, distant voice told him that she had decided to spend the night in town with her mother.

The next morning Elaine came home about ten o'clock, humming a merry little air as she walked down the quiet suburban street. She and Harry had patched things up over the telephone at breakfast-time.

The sun was shining brightly, and she was planning a specially nice dinner for poor Harry that evening. After all, it wasn't the dear boy's fault that he had to work so hard. It was horrible of her to run off and desert him that way. Tonight she would show him how much she loved him. They would have ice cream with hot chocolate sauce, and meringues and chicken salad; and she would buy him a cigar and hide it in his napkin. And the old coffee-um should go back in the glass cabinet.

The cook, with a very grave face, opened the front door.

"Heavens, Emily, what's the matter?" cried Mrs. Bennett.

"Burgled!" said Emily, tragically. "Someone's been an' bruk in the dining-room winder. Footpads, I guess."

Mrs. Bennett gave a little shriek of dismay She ran to the dining room.

One window stood an inch or two open, and one of the panes was broken. She glanced round the room. Nothing was disarranged, but her glance fell on the sideboard.

The coffee-urn was gone!

"Well," she said, "that's very extraordinary. Mr. Bennett slept here last night, and he's a light sleeper. He always locks the windows before he goes to bed. Is anything else missing?"

"The apple pie's gone out o' the ice-box," said Emily.

"Oh, well, that's Mr. Bennett, I'm sure," said Elaine. "I'll call up the police right away, and see if they can do anything. My nice coffee-urn! Why, it's the finest thing we had in the whole house."

Before the police arrived, Mrs. Bennett herself took a careful look round the outside of the house. She found nothing unusual except a cigar butt lying on the ground near the broken window. She picked it up gingerly. A section of the gilt band still adhered to the wrapper. She could read the name, Florona. She carried the fragment into the cellar and threw it into the ash-can.

Two policemen arrived shortly, examined everything, and asked innumerable questions. Mrs. Bennett gave them a careful description of the coffee-urn. They departed, promising to do everything possible to trace it. They said that a piece of silver so large and unusual would not be hard to locate with the aid of the pawnbrokers. Then Mrs. Bennett went upstairs to think.

It seemed very strange that the thieves should take the urn and nothing else, when there were other pieces of silver beside it on the sideboard. She called up Harry, who was horrified to learn of the loss. He had slept right through the night without hearing a sound. He offered to come home if he could do anything to help; but she would not hear of it.

That night Mrs. Bennett had a special little dinner waiting for her husband: his favourite soup, a tender steak, fried potatoes, ice cream with hot chocolate sauce. And after dinner they discussed the theft of the urn.

"I don't understand how it was that you didn't hear anything," said Elaine. "You generally sleep so lightly. Did you sit up late?"

"No," he said; "I sat in the dining room until about ten, eating cheese and apple pie, and smoking a cigar. Then I went to bed——"

"Oh, you just reminded me!" cried Elaine. "I bought you a nice cigar to smoke after your dinner, and I forgot to give it to you."

From the mantelpiece she gave him a cigar with a Florona band.

"Why, isn't that nice!" said he, "That's the kind I always smoke. I didn't think you knew one brand from the other."

"I know more than you think, old man," she said.

When Harry came home the next night, he brought a bulky parcel with him.

"I'm awfully sorry about the urn, Brownie," he said. "I went to see the detectives to-day, and they think there's very little chance of getting it back; so I brought you this to take its place." She opened the package. It was a big China coffee-jug of rose-and-white porcelain, flagrantly out of harmony with her silver and blue china.

"Honey," she said, "I think it's just lovely. It's ever and ever so much nicer than that old urn."

A week later, in the afternoon, the local chief of police called up Mrs. Bennett.

"Come down here to the police station," he said. "We've found your coffee-pot. The most extraordinary thing you ever heard of. We found it buried in a haystack, back of Webster's barn. Why any one should leave it there is more than I know. The thief must have been frightened and hid it. Will you come down and identify it?"

Mrs. Bennett hastened down to the police station. There on the sergeant's table stood the famous urn, the pride of her heart. There was no doubt about it: the initials were there—it was hers. Tarnished and spotted by exposure, it was still the handsomest piece of silver she had ever seen. Involuntarily she gave a cry of delight. Then she hesitated. After all, compared to Harry's happiness and hers, what was a silver urn?

"Oh, captain," she said, "I'm so disappointed. That's not mine! It's very much like it, but it isn't mine."

THE BATTLE OF MANILA ENVELOPES

MR. BIRDLIP was a good old man, of unimpeachable simplicity. He had achieved enormous wealth in an honourable business, and then found (to his mild distress) that the great traffic he had built up conducted itself automatically. He had, in a way, been gently shouldered out of his own nest by the capable men whose fortunes he had made. But his zealous and frugal spirit required some sort of problem to feed upon, and he delighted his heart by owning a newspaper. The Evening Lens was his toy and the child of his dotage.

So the Persian rugs and walnut panelling of his private suite in the huge Birdlip Building saw him rarely. He was supremely happy in the dingy sanctum at the back of the old Lens office, where the hum of the presses and the racket of the city room (which he still, by an innocent misunderstanding, called the "sitting room") delighted his guileless heart. He would sit turning over the pages of each edition as it came upstairs (putting his second finger up to his tongue before he turned each leaf) and poring industriously over the market reports, the comics, and the Woman's Page. With his pink cheeks, his dapper little figure in a brown suit and cream-coloured waistcoat, and his eager, shy, chirping manner, he was very like a robin. Although he was full of gigantic schemes, which he broached naively in the editorial council every now and then, he never wittingly interfered with his editor-in-chief, in whom he had full confidence. But his gentle and jejune mind had a disastrous effect on the paper no less. Almost unconsciously the Lens was written and edited down to his standard, as a roomful of adults will amiably prattle so as to carry along a child in the conversation.

Mr. Birdlip's amazing success in his original field had been due partly to his decent sagacity, honesty, and persistence, and partly to his sheer fortune in finding (at the very outset of his enterprise) several men of rugged ability, who became the pearls in his simple oyster-shell. As a result of this, it had become his fixed mental habit to believe that somewhere, some day, he would encounter the man or men who would make the Lens the greatest newspaper in the country. This, indeed, was his candid ambition, and he never went anywhere without keeping his eyes open for the anticipated messiah.

He was greatly taken by broad primitive effects: when he noticed that a Chicago daily always called itself "The World's Greatest Newspaper" he was marvellously struck by the power of this slogan, and lamented that he had not thought of it first. The question as to whether the slogan were true or not never occurred to him. He liked to have the keynote sentences in the leading editorial emphasized in blackface type, so that there might be no danger of any one's missing the point. Desiring for his beloved sheet "this man's art and that man's scope," as the sonnet puts it, every now and then he thought he had discovered the prodigy, and some new feature would be added to the paper at outrageous expense, only to be quietly shovelled out six months or a year later. In the meantime, the auditor was growing very gray, and even Mr. Birdlip's quick blue eye was sometimes hazed with faint perplexity when he studied the circulation charts. Perhaps it would have been kinder if someone could have told him that a boyhood spent in splitting infinitives is not sufficient training for one to become an Abraham Lincoln of the newspaper business.

As he trotted in and out of the Lens office, with his rosy air of confidence and his disarming simplicity (which made his white hair seem a wanton cruelty on the part of Time, that would wither a man's cells while his mind was still on all fours), Mr. Birdlip was the object of furtive but very sharp study on the part of some cynical journalists whom he hired. It was a genuine amazement to Sanford, the dramatic critic, that the owner was so entirely unaware of his (Sanford's) abilities, which certainly (he thought) called for a salary of more than sixty dollars a week. Sanford often meditated about this, and not entirely in secret. In fact, it was generally admitted among the younger members of the staff, when they gathered at Ventriloquo's for lunch, that the Old Man was immaculately ignorant of all phases of the newspaper business. While the spaghetti and mushrooms cheered the embittered gossips, merry and quaint were the quips sped toward the unsuspecting target. Sanford's private grievance was that though for over a year he had been doing signed critiques of plays, which were really spirited and honest, not once had the Old Man condescended to mention them, or to show any sign of uttering an Ecce Homo in his direction. As far as he was concerned, he felt that the weekly battle of Manila Envelopes was a conspicuous rout, and he frequently rehearsed the exact tone in which he would some day say to the managing editor: "You may fire when ready, Gridley." Little did Sanford realize that the only time Mr. Birdlip had attempted to read the "Exits and

Entrances" column he had met the name of Æschylus, had faltered, and retreated upon the syndicated sermon by the Rev. Frank Crane.

"I saw 'Ruddigore' the other evening," said Sanford to his cronies, as they called for a second round of coffee. "There's a line in it that describes old Birdie fore, aft, and amidships. Something like this: 'He is that particular variety of good old man to whom the truth is always a refreshing novelty'."

They complauded. Rightly or wrongly, these high-spirited and sophisticated young men had decided that Mr. Birdlip's naïveté was so refreshingly complete that it gave them an aesthetic pleasure to contemplate it. It had the exquisite beauty of any absolute perfection. Their employer's latest venture, which had been to pay $200,000 for the exclusive right to publish and syndicate the mysterious formulae of a leading Memory Course, had shocked them very greatly.

It touched them in a tender spot to know that there had been all that money lying round the office, unused, which was now to be squandered (as they put it) on charlatanry, when they felt that they might just as well have had some of it.

"The Old Man is always looking for some special stunt, and trying to discover someone on the outside," said one. "He can't see the material right under his nose."

"It's really rather pathetic: he's crazy to get out a great newspaper, but he hasn't the faintest idea how to do it."

"Yes, give him credit for sincerity. It isn't just circulation he wants."

"Circulation's easy enough, if that's what you're after. The three builders of circulation are Sordid, Sensational, and Sex—"

"And the greatest of these is Sex."

"Oh, he's decent enough. He won't pander."

"He panders to stupidity. He's fallen for this Memory bunk. And when he finds that's a flivver, he'll try something else, equally fatuous. He's making the old Lens ridiculous."

They smoked awhile, meditatively.

"What I would like to figure out," said Sanford, "is some way of

94

making an impression on the Old Man. I've got to get more money. The trouble—some part of it is, I feel instinctively that he and I live in different worlds. We hardly even talk the same language. Well, there's no chance of his learning my way of thinking; so I suppose I'll have to learn his."

"He's the man who puts the nil in the Manila envelope," said one of the others.

"As far as we are concerned, yes. But there's plenty of the stuff going round on Fridays for the kind of people he understands."

"He seems to be an absent-minded old bird. When I talk to him, it's as though I were trying to speak through a fog."

"It looks to me as though his mind had overstayed its leave of absence."

"He likes the kind of men who, as he says, 'have both feet on the ground'."

"Yes, but you've got to have at least one foot in the air if you're going to get anywhere."

"See here," said the literary editor, who was more tolerant than the others. "What's the use of panning the Old Man? He's trying to put the paper over, just as hard as we are. Maybe harder. But he doesn't know. And I believe he knows he doesn't know. I think the chief trouble is, they all knuckle down to him so. They're scared of him. They think the only way they can hold their jobs is by agreeing with him. If someone could only put him wise——"

"But how can you put him wise? He doesn't see anything unless it's laid out for him in a strip cartoon or a full-page ad. The kind of thing that interests him is the talk he hears in a Pullman smoker or club car."

"That's a fact. You know he always says he likes to go travelling, because he picks up ideas from people on the train. 'Of course I place you! Mr. Mowbray Monk of Seattle. And is your Rotary Club still rotating?' That kind of talk."

"I think you're right," said Sanford. "He doesn't see us because we have too much protective colouring. We are only the patient drudges. We don't talk that Pullman palaver about Big Business. We've got to learn to talk his language. What is that phrase of

Bacon's—we've got to bring ourselves home to his business and bosom——"

"Let's get back to the office," said the disillusioned literary editor. "That's the way to bring home the bacon."

A few days later Sanford was at his desk, clipping and pasting press agents' flimsies for the Saturday Theatre Page. This was a task which he hated above all others, and he was meditating sourly on the scarcity of truth in human affairs. At this moment Mr. Birdlip happened to pass along the corridor outside the editorial rooms. Sanford heard him say:

"Miss Flaccus, will you get me a seat in the club car, ten o'clock train to-morrow? I've got to run over to New York to take lunch with Mr. Montaigne."

Sanford put down his shears, relit his pipe, and began to pursue a fugitive idea round the suburbs of his mind. Presently he drew out his check book from a drawer and did some calculating on a sheet of paper. "A hundred dollars," he said to himself. "I guess it's worth it."

The following morning, dressed in a new suit and with shoes freshly burnished, Sanford was at the terminal twenty minutes before train time. With him was a young man carrying a leather portfolio. To observe the respectful demeanour of this young man, no one would have suspected that he was Sanford's young brother-in-law, rejoicing in cutting his classes at college for a day's masquerading. Sanford bought some cigars (a form of smoking which he detested) and carefully removed the bands from all but one of them.

Presently Mr. Birdlip appeared, cheerfully trotting up the stairs. Sanford and his companion followed discreetly. As Mr. Birdlip went through the gate, they were close behind. Entering the club car, Mr. Birdlip sat down and opened a morning paper. Sanford and his companion were prompt to take the two adjoining seats. Sanford began to look over System and Printers' Ink, and perhaps his interest in these vigorous journals was not wholly unfeigned, for it was the first time he had studied them. The young man beside him drew out a mass of papers from his leather bag, and in a moment of stillness just before the train started said in a clear voice:

"Pardon, sir, but there is some important dictation here that ought to be attended to."

Sanford assumed the air of a man wearied with tremendous affairs. .

"Very well, what comes first?"

"The New York Budget has wired for an answer in regard to their proposition."

Sanford blew a luxurious whiff of smoke. "Take this letter: My dear Mr. Ralston. Replying to your inquiries as to whether I would be willing to take charge of the editorial page of the Budget for a few months, to put the paper on its feet, I am willing to consider the matter, and would be pleased to discuss it with you if you will run over to see me. I am very busy just now, and could not possibly undertake the work for some weeks. I have been retained in an advisory capacity by a big Western syndicate which was badly in need of some circulation building; and until I can put their paper up to a half-million figure I have not much spare time. Their paper has gone up a couple of hundred thousand since I mapped out a campaign for them, but I would not feel justified in discontinuing my services to them until these gains are properly consolidated. I will be in my office at ten o'clock next Tuesday morning if you care to see me. Very truly yours."

Mr. Birdlip was hidden behind his paper, but something in the angle at which the sheets were held led Sanford to believe that the old gentleman was listening.

"Very well, Edwards," he said. "What's next?"

"Here's this letter from Lord Southpeak of the London Gazette asking if he can see you when he comes over next month."

"Cable Southpeak I shall be very happy to see him if he gets here before the fifteenth. I am going on my vacation then."

The attentive Edwards scribbled rapidly in his notebook.

"Just pick out the most urgent stuff," said Sanford. "I don't care to bother with anything that isn't really pressing. I've got an important conference on in New York to-day, and I want to keep my mind clear. Blackwit of the Associated Press has asked me to say a few words to his directors on 'Journalism as a Function of Public Conscience'."

Edwards ran rapidly through an imposing mass of documents.

"That long-distance call from the Chicago Vox," he said. "You promised to give Mr. Groton some word this morning."

"Call him up when we get to Penn. Station," said Sanford. "Tell him I can't give him any decision yet awhile. Tell him that loyalty to my own city will keep me there for some time. You might tell him that I believe the Lens has great possibilities if properly handled. I should not care to build up the property of a Chicago paper while there is a chance of the Lens becoming the great evening paper of the East."

"Yes, sir," said Edwards, jotting down what, might pass for stenography.

The train was running smoothly through level green country, and Mr. Birdlip laid down his paper on his lap. Sanford was ready to catch his eye.

"Good morning, Mr. Birdlip," he said, genially.

"Good morning," said the owner of the Lens, whose bright gaze exhibited a lively tincture of interest.

"Here are the typed notes of your remarks on 'Newspaper Circulation as a Byproduct of the Multiplication Table'," said Edwards, in a loud voice.

"You can let those wait," said Sanford, carelessly. "I don't want to be bothered with anything else this morning. Give me a memorandum of anything that needs to be attended to when we get to New York." He turned to Mr. Birdlip. "I find that in these busy days one has to attend to some of one's work even on the train. It is about the only place where one is never interrupted."

"Did I hear you say something about Circulation?" said Mr. Birdlip. "Are you specially interested in that problem?"

"I have given it a good deal of thought," said Sanford. "But I would hardly dignify it by calling it a problem. It is perfectly simple. It is purely a matter of taking the right attitude toward it. So many newspaper proprietors regard it merely as a problem in addition. Now it should be considered rather as a matter of multiplication. Instead of trying to add ten to your figures, why not multiply by ten? The result is so much more satisfactory."

This sounded so plausible that Mr. Birdlip felt ashamed to ask how it was to be done.

"Will you have a cigar, sir?" asked Sanford, handing out the only one with a band on it. Mr. Birdlip accepted it, and looked as though he were about to ask a question. Sanford went on rapidly.

"Speaking of circulation," he said, "when I am consulted I am always surprised to note that newspaper proprietors are so prone to view the matter merely as a question of distribution; of—well, of merchandising," he added, as his eye fell upon that word in his copy of System. "Indeed it rests upon quite another basis. The essence of merchandising" (he repeated the word with relish, noting its soothing effect on his employer) "is what?"

He made a dramatic pause, and Mr. Birdlip, carried away, wondered what indeed was the essence.

"The essence of merchandising," said Sanford (he smote the arm of his chair, and leaned forward in emphasis), "and by merchandising I mean of course in the modern sense, merchandising on a big scale, is nothing but Confidence. Confidence, an impalpable thing, a state of mind. Now, sir, what is it that upbuilds circulation? It is Public Confidence. The assurance on the part of the public that the newspaper is reliable. It is a secret and inviolable conviction on the part of the reader that the integrity and enterprise of the paper are beyond cavil, in other words, unimpeachable. In order to create the Will-to-Purchase on the part of the prospect, in order to beget that desirable state of mind, there must be a state of mind in the paper itself. Note that word Mind. Now what is the Mind of the paper? I always ask every newspaper owner who consults me, what is the Mind of his paper?"

Without waiting for Mr. Birdlip to be embarrassed by his inability to answer this question, the ecstatic Sanford continued:

"The Mind of the paper is, of course, the Editorial Department. How subtle, how delicate, how momentous, is that function of commenting on the great affairs of the world! As I said in an address to a Rotary club recently, of what use to have all the mechanical perfections ever invented unless your editors are the right men? Walter Whitman, the efficiency engineer, said: 'Produce great persons: the rest follows.' That is the kind of production that counts most. Get great personalities for your editors, and watch the circulation rise. Of course the right kind of editors must be very highly paid."

This was a strange doctrine to Mr. Birdlip, who never read the editorial page of his own paper, and secretly wondered how the editors found so much to write about.

"The great error that so many newspaper owners make," said Sanford, sonorously, "is to think of their product as they would of any other article of commerce which is turned out day by day, in standardized units, from a factory. A newspaper is not standardized. It is born anew every issue. It is not a manufacturing routine that puts it together: it is a human organism, built up out of human brains. Every unit is different. It depends not primarily on machinery but on human personalities. I cannot understand why it is that newspaper owners yearn for the finest and most modern presses, and yet are often content to staff their journals with second-rate men."

"I agree with you," said Mr. Birdlip. "It is all a question of getting the right man. That is one reason why I am so fond of travelling; I always meet up with new ideas. Now, sir (I am sorry I do not know your name, for your face is rather familiar; I think I must have met you at some Rotary club), you seem to me a man of forceful and aggressive character. You are the kind of man I should like to have on the Lens, I heard you mention the paper to your secretary awhile back; you must be interested in it."

Sanford was perfectly cool. "I might consider it," he said.

"I think you would find the Lens a pleasant paper to work on," said Mr. Birdlip. "I flatter myself that the staff is a capable one, for the most part."

"I should insist on being given a free hand," said Sanford. "Perhaps the position of circulation manager——?"

"Let me think a moment," said Mr. Birdlip. "I suppose I ought to visit with my editor-in-chief before firing any one to make room for you. But I must say I like the way you talk, straight from the shoulder, like that Dr. Cranium, you know. That's the sort of stuff we need."

"Right!" cried Sanford. "If you always talk straight from the shoulder, you'll never talk through your hat."

Mr. Birdlip relished this impromptu aphorism. "Well, now, let me see," he said, pondering. "The editor-in-chief, the managing editor, the editorial writers—they're all pretty good men."

100

"Of course I shouldn't care for a merely routine position," said Sanford. "The only position I would consider would be one in which I could really build up circulation for you." He was wondering inwardly whether to stand out for a ten thousand salary.

"Quite so," said Mr. Birdlip. "I think I have it. How would you care to run a column? 'Straight From the Shoulder'—wouldn't that be a fine title?"

"Fine!" said Sanford, but not without a secret shudder. Still, he thought, gold can assuage anything; and he reflected on the rich, sedentary, and care-free life of a syndicated philosopher.

"Very well," said the owner. "I've been looking around for a man with both feet on the ground——"

("Both feet on the pay envelope is my idea," said Sanford to himself.)

"And I think you're just the man I want. There's only one place in the paper I can think of that really needs a change. There's a fellow on the staff called Sanford, runs a kind of column, terrible stuff. I don't think he amounts to much. Now why couldn't you take his job?"

Sanford has never forgiven his brother-in-law for that curious strangled sound he emitted.

THE CLIMACTERIC

MR. EUSTACE VEAL was a manufacturer of cuspidors. His beautiful factory was one of the finest of its kind, equipped with complete automatic sprinklers, wire-glass windows, cafeteria on the top floor, pensions for superannuated employees, rosewood directors' dining room, mottoes from Orison Swett Marden on the weekly pay envelopes, and a clever young man in tortoise-shell spectacles hired at eighty dollars a week to write the house-organ (which was called El Cuspidorado).

Mr. Veal lived in the exclusive and clean-shaven suburb of Mandrake Park, where he had built a stucco mansion with Venetian blinds, a croquet lawn with a revolving spray on it on hot days, and a mansard butler. Here Mrs. Veal and the two Veal girls, Dora and Petunia, led the blameless life of the embonpoint classes. The electric lights in the bedrooms were turned on promptly at ten o'clock every night, except on the sixteen winter evenings when the Veals occupied their box at the opera. During "Rigoletto" or "Pagliacci" the uncomplaining Mr. Veal would sit in silence with his head against the thick red velvet curtain at the back of the box, thinking up new ways to get an order for ten thousand nickel-plated seamless number 13's from the Pullman Company.

Mr. Veal, hampered as he was by the restrictions of success, was still full of the enjoyment of life. He had written a little brochure on "The Cuspidor: Its Use and Abuse Since the Times of the Pharaohs," which was very well spoken of in the trade. A morocco-bound copy lay on the console table in Mrs. Veal's salon. It was he who invented the papier-maché spittoon, and the collapsible paper "companion" for travelling salesmen. It was he who had presented a solid silver spittoon de luxe to the King of Siam when that worthy visited the United States. And it was his idea, too, to name the beautiful shining brass model, especially recommended for hotel lobbies, El Cuspidorado. This was a stroke of imaginative genius, and several rival manufacturers wept because they had not thought of it first.

The spittoon magnate's habits were regular and sane. He rose by alarm clock at seven. He bathed, shaved, brushed his teeth with the vertical motion recommended by the toothbrush advertisers, breakfasted on cereal and cream and poached eggs, with one cup of strong coffee; walked leisurely to the station, bought a paper, and

102

caught the 8.13 train. He avoided the other men who wanted him to sit with them, took the fifth chair on the left-hand side of the smoking car, and just as the train started he lit his first cigar. His commutation ticket was always ready for the conductor to punch. He never kept others waiting, just as he hated to be kept waiting himself. After his ticket had been punched and put back into an alligator-hide pocketbook, he opened the paper and studied it faithfully until the train got to the terminal.

At the factory Mr. Veal's routine was equally well-ordered and uniform. At nine o'clock he reached his private office, greeted his secretary, and ran over the morning mail, which had been opened and lay on his desk. Then he went through his dictation, which was carefully (even if not grammatically) accomplished. The sales reports for the preceding day were brought to him. Then he discussed any matters requiring attention with his department heads, calling them in one by one. At a quarter after twelve he walked up to the Manufacturers' Club for lunch, after which he played one game of pool.

He was back at the office by half-past two, and gave his passionate and devoted attention to the salivary needs of the nation until five o'clock. He caught the 5.23 train back to Mandrake Park, sitting on the right-hand side of the smoker where the setting sun would not dazzle on his newspaper.

But one day, about the time of the March equinox, when young ladies put furry pussywillows on their typewriter desks, and bank tellers crack the shells of spring jokes through the brass railings, Mr. Veal's behaviour was so peculiar as to cause anxiety among his associates.

He had ridden on the train as usual, without showing any abnormal symptoms. But when he was next observed, walking down Vincent Street, there was a red spot on his cheekbones and his expression was savage. He entered a haberdasher's shop and asked to see some neckties. When the clerk put out a tray of silk scarves in rich, sober colours, such as are commonly worn by successful and middle-aged merchants, Mr. Veal swore and dashed them aside.

"Good Lord!" he cried, "I'm not going to a funeral! Things like that are worn by Civil War veterans. What do you think I am, seventy years old? Give me something with some snap to it!"

And he chose a lemon-tinted cravat with vorticist patterns of brown and purple. He tore off the dark gray tie he had on and substituted the gaudy new one.

At the next corner he passed a shoe-shop. He hesitated a moment at the plate-glass window, then he entered and glared at the brisk young puppet who came forward with a smirk. He displayed his elastic-sided boots of the floorwalker type (which he had worn for years on account of his corns) and asked to have them removed. When they were off his feet he threw them to the other end of the long, narrow room. "I want some russet shoes with cloth tops," he said. "And some silk socks to match, the kind the men wear in the magazine ads."

When he left the shop, his feet might have been taken for those of Charley Chaplin, or of an assistant advertising manager of a department store.

Mr. Veal reached his office nearly two hours late, and one of his office boys was instantly discharged for asking him whom he wanted to see. Indeed, in a new suit of violent black-and-white checks, and with a crush hat of velvety substance, he was almost unrecognizable. As he passed through the filing department a hush fell over the young ladies there. His secretary, looking nervously from her corner outside the private office, felt a tingling scherzo run up and down the keyboard of her spine. Never before had she seen Mr. Veal wear flowers in his buttonhole, and as he swung the door of his office behind him, she sniffed the vibrating air. In the rich wake of cigar-fragrance always exhaled by her employer her sharp nostrils detected a new tang—the sweet scent of mignonette. Heavens! Was Mr. Veal using perfume?

Miss Stafford was an acute young woman. She had long been waiting the adroit moment to push her employer for a raise, which was indeed due her. She determined that this was the psychological day. When the sign of the Ram is ascendant in the zodiac, let employers tremble. This is when even the most faithful and long-enduring wage-earner dreams seditiously of a fatter manila envelope. Miss Stafford's typewriter had sung like a zither for a number of years, she had orchestrated many curious harmonies on it, and now she had reached the point where she was almost as indispensable to the business as Mr. Veal himself. She was carrying what the efficiency dopesters call the peak load.

The buzzer buzzed, and Miss Stafford hastened to the private office, nerving herself to throw cantilevers across the Rubicon.

To her surprise, Mr. Veal, instead of sitting glowering over the morning mail, was standing by the window, throwing a paper-weight in the air and failing to catch it. The sunlight blazing through the large windows seemed to surround his emphatic clothes with a prismatic fringe. To her amazement, instead of the customary brief and reserved greeting, he said:

"Hullo, Miss Stafford. Great weather, eh? Sorry I'm late, but I just couldn't keep my schedule this morning. Went out to buy myself some golf clubs. I think I'd better take up the game, don't you?"

He made a swing at an imaginary golf ball, and slipped on the polished floor, nearly falling down. He recovered himself.

"Here's some flowers for you," he said, taking a bunch of daffodils from the desk. "Daffy-down-dillies, as the poets call 'em. Lovely flowers, hey? Now comes in the sweet of the year. What ho!"

He advanced toward her, and for one extraordinary moment she thought he was about to chuck her under the chin.

"Ask Mr. Foster to come in," he said.

"Mr. Veal," she said, nervously, "there's just one thing—I wanted to ask you about, my salary, don't you think, er, I think, it seems to me about time I had a raise. I've been here——"

"Bless my soul," he said. "I never thought of it. Why, of course, you're right. Miss Stafford, how old would you say I am?"

Miss Stafford knew perfectly well that he was fifty-five, but she had learned the cunning of all women who have to manage men, whether those men be husbands, employers, or ticket scalpers.

"Why, Mr. Veal, in a good light and in your new suit, I should say about thirty-nine."

"What are you getting now, Miss Stafford?"

"Thirty dollars."

"Tell Mr. Mason to double it."

The feminine mind moves in rapid zigzags, and Miss Stafford's first conscious and coherent thought was of a certain woollen sports suit she had seen in a window on Vincent Street marked $50.00.

"And by the way," said Mr. Veal, "when you see Mr. Mason, tell him I've got a new motto for next week's pay envelopes. Here it is; I found it in the paper this morning. I don't know who wrote it— better have him credit it to Orison Swett Marden."

He handed her a slip of paper, on which he had copied out:

> *Though I look old, yet I am strong and lusty;*
> *For in my youth I never did apply*
> *Hot and rebellious liquors in my blood:*
> *Nor did not with unbashful forehead woo*
> *The means of weakness and debility.*
> *—Orison Swett Marden (?)*

"Before you call Mr. Foster," said the secretary, "Mr. Schmaltz of the Pullman Company is here to see you; he arrived just before you came in. He says he wants to place a large order for the cuspidorados."

"Send him in," said Mr. Veal, chuckling. "Hello, Schmaltz," he cried, as the customer entered. "How's this for weather?"

"Great stuff!" said Schmaltz. "Makes us old fellows feel almost young again, doesn't it?"

Mr. Veal's face grew dark. He aged ten years in the instant. He pointed morosely to a chair.

"Mr. Veal," said the other, "we want to place an order for ten thousand of the cuspidorados. Can you give us the old price?"

"I can not," said Mr. Veal, shortly. "Materials have gone to the sky. I can't give you the—the old price. I'll give you a young price, a very young one indeed, based on the present state of the market. Eighteen and a quarter cents is the best I can do."

Mr. Schmaltz raised racial hands. "Heavens!" he said, "you used to let us have them for fourteen and a half. Why, in the old days——"

Mr. Veal pounded the desk with his fist.

"If you use that world old again, I'll assassinate you with a dish of ham!" he roared. "Great pigs' knuckles, what do you think this is, a home for the aged?"

After Mr. Schmaltz had gone Mr. Veal sent for Foster, the foreman of the manufacturing department.

"Well," he said, "how about those machines?"

"Mr. Veal," said Foster, "we'll have to replace at least six of those Victor stampers. They're so old they simply can't do the work. You know when one of those machines is over five years old——"

Mr. Veal was pointing to the door.

"Get out!" he said.

At lunch-time Mr. Veal went up to the club as usual. Swinging up the street, in the bright sun and pellucid air, he felt quite cheerful, and stopped to buy himself a rhinoceros cane. In the dining room of the club he met Edwards, and they sat down together.

"Hello, old man," said Edwards. "You're looking chipper for a veteran. Played any golf yet this year?"

"I don't play," said Mr. Veal.

"Don't you? That's a mistake. It's the only game for us older fellows. Of course we can't score like the youngsters; but still we can get round and have a deal of fun——"

Mr. Veal clenched his fists. Spilling his soup, he leaped up and rushed from the room. He seized his coat and hat, forgetting the new cane, and fled to the nearest Turkish bath.

And all because, when going downstairs in the railway terminal that morning, he had heard a man behind him say to another:

"There goes Veal! He's beginning to look old, isn't he?"

It was the first time in his life Mr. Veal had heard the damnable adjective applied to himself in earnest.

Wait until your turn comes!

107

PUNCH AND JUDY

WHEN Judy Cronin first saw the topless towers of Manhattan rising into the lilac vagueness of a foggy winter morning she passed into a numb and frightened daze. Standing on the steerage deck of the Celtic, she peered tremulously at those fantastic impossible profiles of stone. Perhaps you don't know what it is to be thrown, ignorant and timid, into a place where everything is utterly strange—particularly a place as huge, violent, and hasty as New York. Judy, aged twenty-one, from a little village near Queenstown, was incapable of distinguishing, in the roaring voice of the city, that undertone of helpful kindness that is really there. On the same steamer came the widow of a famous Irish recusant and hungerstriker, and there were ten thousand people massed in West Street to cheer her. Judy heard the shouts of the crowd, and saw the lines of policemen on the pier. There was some of that quiet but menacing scuffling with which the various branches of the English-speaking world show their esteem for each other. Judy was not familiar with that definition of a patriot as one who makes trouble for his harmless fellow-citizens; but it looked as though she was blundering into some more of the tribulations they had had at home.

At last her sister Connie found her, sitting white and miserable on her very small trunk, clutching her imitation-silver coin-purse. Connie had been in New York for a couple of years, and it gave her a homesick throb to see that coin-purse—one of those little metal pocketbooks with slots to hold gold sovereigns and half-sovereigns. Father Daly had given it to Judy, years ago, but it had never had gold in the little sockets until Connie sent over the passage money to bring Judy to New York.

The city flashed by like a current-events film. Judy found herself in a friendly lodging-house in Brooklyn, kept by an Irishwoman who had been kind to Connie. Her sister then explained matters. Her own employers, with whom she had a position too good to abandon, had arranged to go South for the latter part of the winter. They had already delayed leaving so that Connie could meet her sister and get her settled. They had given Connie a few days' holiday for that purpose.

Therefore Judy must get a place as soon as possible. And that very afternoon the sisters (Judy still in a kind of dreadful dream) went to the office of a Brooklyn newspaper to insert an advertisement.

A great many people were watching the Situations Wanted columns, and the next evening, at supper-time, Mrs. Leland called up the lodging-house number, which had been given in the ad. Connie went to the telephone. Mrs. Leland had a pleasant voice and "talked like gentry", Connie said. She lived in Heathwood, Long Island, which is some twenty miles from town, and wanted a nurse to take care of two children. Connie agreed to take Judy out to Heathwood the next morning, to see if they could come to terms. Judy was inexperienced, but Mrs. Leland liked her looks. In short: by the time Judy had been in America three days, she was installed at Mrs. Leland's home in the country; and a few days later Connie had gone off to Florida.

Now Judy was really very fortunate in these random proceedings, for she had found a good home under an exceptionally kind and understanding mistress. And therefore perhaps it was unreasonable of her to be so unhappy. But no one has ever demonstrated that human affairs are much controlled by reason. Judy was dumbly and piteously miserable. She was homesick and lonely, and half-mad with strangeness. She was not really slow-witted; but the confusion of her spirits put her into a kind of black stupor. Everything was uncouth to her: steam heat, electric light, gas-stove, telephone— even the alarm clock in her bedroom. Not knowing how to turn off her radiator, and having the simple person's distrust of opening windows in a strange place, the first few nights she was sick with heat and suffocation. In her sleep she cried out indistinguishable words about being shot. In spite of Mrs. Leland's patient tuition, she made every possible kind of mistake. The children, with the quickness of youth, realized her inexperience and uncertainty, and played a thousand impish pranks. Mrs. Leland could see that the girl had been through distresses at home, and kept the evening papers, with their headlines about Ireland, out of sight. But one evening, in the kitchen, Judy came upon a Sunday rotogravure section with pictures of burnt streets in Cork. The look of the people in those photographs went through her heart. The men wearing caps, the women in shawls, something even in the shape of trouser legs and heavy shoes, reminded Judy how far she was from all that she understood. It's the little things you take for granted at home that come back to hurt you when you're away. That night, sitting in her bedroom next the nursery, she shook herself ill with sobs.

One who might have helped her greatly took pains to add to her bewilderment. Hattie, Mrs. Leland's coloured cook, a retainer of long standing, was sharply disgruntled at this new addition to the household. Jealousy was the root of Hattie's irritation, and it shot up a rapid foliage of poison ivy. The previous nurse, a bosom friend of Hattie's own race, had been discharged in December for incompetence. Moreover, Hattie had not forgotten poor naïve Judy's startled look when they first encountered. Judy had hardly seen a coloured person before, and was honestly alarmed. Hattie, though loyal to Mrs. Leland in her own primitive fashion, deeply resented this interloper. The invasion proved that Mrs. Leland was no longer entirely dependent on the particular clique of Heathwood coloured society in which Hattie moved. The cook's logic was narrow but rigorous. The sooner the intruder could be discouraged out of the house, the sooner the Black Hussars (as Heathwood ladies called the coloured colony on whom they largely relied for assistance) would resume undivided sway. Mrs. Leland had had a Polish girl as a stop-gap for a few days after the coloured nurse left; and observing the cook's demeanour toward this unfortunate, Mr. Leland had remarked that Hattie was working for a black Christmas.

So Hattie, who was sharp-tongued and very capable, hectored Judy whenever she entered the kitchen, and by all the black arts at her command (which were many) added to the girl's distress. Judy, in spite of her mistress's kindness, grew more and more wretched. As Mr. Leland said in private (pursuing the train of his previous pun), the maids were black and blue. Mrs. Leland, much goaded by domestic management and the care of a very small baby, began to wonder whether she had not added another child to look after rather than lightening her burdens. And then she saw that Judy was on the verge of nervous collapse. She tried to hearten the girl by giving her an extra holiday. Judy was given some money, packed off to the station in a taxi, and sent on her maiden trip to town in the hope that city sights and shop windows would revive her interest in life. Mrs. Flaherty, the lodging-house lady in Brooklyn, was telephoned to, and promised to send her small boy to meet the girl at the station.

It happened to be the eve of the genial Saint Valentine's Day. Shop windows were gay with pleasantly exaggerated symbols of his romantic power. Winter afternoons in the city are cruel to the unfortunate, for the throng of the streets the light and lure of the scene, make loneliness all the worse if there is trouble in your heart.

Judy sat in the waiting room of the Long Island terminal in Brooklyn, and tears were on her face. She had somehow missed Mrs. Flaherty's lad. Then she had tried to find her way to the lodging-house, but grew more and more frightened and bewildered as she strayed. Giving that up, she had gone into a movie, and there, for a while, she had been happy. The favourites of the screen are the true internationalists: they speak a language, crude though it often is, which is known from Brooklyn to Bombay. But then pictures were shown of scenes in Ireland. She came out with cold hands, and wandered vaguely along the streets until dusk. Finally, in despair, she groped back to the station at Flatbush Avenue, and sat forlornly on a bench, too weary and sorry even to ask how to get home.

With the unerring instinct of the stranger for choosing the wrong place, she had blundered into the downstairs station, by the train-gates, missing the waiting room above where departures are duly announced by orotund men in blue and silver. In that chilly cavern she sat, dumbly watching the press of homeward commuters laden with parcels and papers. Red signboards clattered up and down over the iron gates, and she puzzled doubtfully over such names as Speonk, and Far Rockaway. The last somehow recalled a nursery rhyme and made her feel even more lost and homesick. Occasionally, with a gentle groan and rumble, an electric train slid up to the railing and stared at her with two fierce hostile eyes. The soda fountain in the corner was doing a big business: timidly she went over, feeling cold, and asked for tea. To her amazement, there were no hot drinks to be had. The people, all gulping iced mixtures, stared at her curiously. Sure, this is a mad country, she thought. The clock telling the time was the only thing she could properly understand.

So it was the clock, at last, that brought her to startled action. It was getting late. A tall, good-looking fellow in a blue uniform came out of a room at the back of the station, carrying two lighted lanterns. He halted not far from where she was sitting, and compared his watch with the Western Union clock. Of all the hundreds she had seen, he was the first who looked easily questionable. With a sudden impulse Judy got up, clutching her coin-purse.

"If you please, where will I be after taking the train to Heathwood?" she said, nervously.

"Heathwood? The 6:18 makes Heathwood. Right over there, the gate's just opening. Change at Jamaica."

111

He looked down at her, wondering but kindly. He was puzzled at the frightened way she was staring at his coat-collar; he could hardly have guessed that to wet eyes the embroidered letters had at first seemed to be liar. Her puny, pinched face was streaked with tears, the red knitted muffler made her pallor even whiter. The little imitation fur trimmings on her coat sleeves and collar were worn and shabby.

"Thank you," she said, blindly, and started off for the wrong gate.

"Hey!" he called, and overtook her in a few long strides. "This way, miss. Got your ticket?"

In a sudden panic she opened her purse, and could not find it.

"Oh, surely I've lost it," she cried. "Where's the booking office?"

"The booking office?" he said. "D'you mean the news-stand? Here you are." He picked up the ticket, which she had dropped in her nervousness.

"That's all right," he said, encouragingly. "This train, over here. I'm one of the crew. I'll see you get there. Don't worry."

He escorted her through the gate, and found her a seat on the train, beside a stout commuter half buried in parcels.

"Now you stay right here," he said. "I'll tell you when we get to Jamaica, and show you the Heathwood train." He smiled genially, and left her.

Judy got out her wet handkerchief and wiped her face. As the train ran through the tunnel, she wished she had been on the inside of the seat, for the dark window would have been useful as a mirror. "He saw me crying," she kept repeating to herself. The man beside her blanketed himself with a newspaper, and the pile of packages on his knees kept sliding over onto her lap, but she was oblivious. She was thinking of the tall man in blue with the queer cap. How kind he had been. The first real kindness she had met in all that nightmare afternoon.

Presently he came through the car. She could see him far down the aisle, leaning courteously over each seat. At first she thought he was just saying a friendly word to all the passengers. Sure, that's like him, she said to herself: he has a grand way with him. Then she saw

112

that he was punching tickets with a silver clipper. Glory, it's the Guard himself, she thought. I wonder will he speak to me again?

The man beside her thrust an arm out from his mass of bundles and held a large oblong of red-striped cardboard across in front of her face. This reminded Judy of her own ticket, which was so different from her neighbour's that she worried for a moment lest it should not be valid. Here was her friend, bending above her with a smile.

"Everything all right?" he said. "The next stop's Jamaica. That's where you get off. Watch for me at this door, and I'll show you the Heath-wood train." Click, click: the two tickets were punched, and he went on. Judy shut up her coin purse with a snap, and began to notice the hat worn by the lady in the seat in front.

At Jamaica she found him in the vestibule, his head overtopping the pushing crowd. "This way," he said, and led her quickly across the platform. "Jack," he said to the brakeman on the other train, "tell this lady when you get to Heathwood."

"Well, Judy," said Mrs. Leland when her nursemaid got back to the house. "How much better you look! Did you have a good time?"

"Oh, a grand time," said Judy. Her face had a touch of colour and indeed even her awkward bog-trotting gait seemed lighter and more sprightly. "That's good," said her mistress. "You'd better run down and get some supper before Hattie puts everything away. You can put Jack to bed after you've had something to eat."

"Pretty late for supper," grumbled Hattie, as Judy came into the kitchen. "Doan' you think I got nothing to do but wait on you?"

"I'll get my own supper," said Judy, politely. "Don't you bother."

"You've got a head on your shoulders," said Hattie, banging some dishes on to the kitchen table. "Whyn't you use it and get back on time?"

"The black banshee's up in arms again," said Judy to herself. "I'll hold my peace."

"That's the trouble with foreigners," growled Hattie. "They ain't got no sense. These Irish micks come over here, puttin' on airs, where nobody wants 'em."

Judy's sallow cheek began to burn a darker tint.

113

"Ah, nabocklish!" she said. "There's somebody loves me, at any rate."

She hurried through supper, and ran upstairs to put Jack to bed. The six-year-old was amusing himself by snapping open and shut something that gleamed in the lamplight.

"Here!" she said. "What are you doing with Judy's purse?"

Jack looked up in surprise. It was the first time that he had heard that note of command in the meek Judy's voice.

"I found it on your bureau," he said.

"Well, leave it be, darlin'." She took it from him. "Glory above, what's become of——?"

She fell on her knees on the floor and began searching.

"Ah, here, 'tis!" she cried, gladly. From the rug she picked up a tiny red cardboard heart, and replaced it carefully in one of the sockets of her purse.

"What is it?" said Jack, yawning.

"Sure, it's my Valentine!" said Judy. "It ain't many girls that gets a Valentine from a big handsome man like that the first time he sees them."

I have often wondered how many of the Long Island trainmen use a heart-shaped punch.

REFERRED TO THE AUTHOR

YES, "Obedience" is a fine play. I'm glad they've revived it. Did you know that the first time it was produced, Morgan Edwards played the part of Dunbar? It's rather an odd story.

I never think of Edwards without remembering the dark, creaky stairs in that boarding-house on Seventy-third Street. That was where I first met him. We had a comical habit of always encountering on the stairs. We would pass with that rather ridiculous murmur and sidling obeisance of two people who don't know each other but want to be polite. I was interested in him at once. Even on the shadowy stairway I could see that he had a fine head, and there was something curiously attractive about his pale, preoccupied face. There was a touch of the unworldly about him, and a touch of the tragic, too. You know how you divine things about people. "He has troubles of his own" was the banal phrase that came into my mind. Also there was something queerly familiar about him. I wondered if I had seen Him before, or only imagined him. I was busy writing, at that time, and my mind was peopled with energetic phantoms. The thought struck me that perhaps he was someone I had invented for a story, but had never given life to. I wondered, was this pale and rather reproachful spectre going to haunt me until the tale was written? At any rate, whatever the story was, I had forgotten it.

One day, as I creaked up the first flight, I saw that he was standing at the head of the stairs, waiting for me to pass. A door was open behind him, and there was light enough to see him clearly. Tall, thin, beautifully shaven on a fine angular jaw that would not be easy to shave, I was surprised to see an air of sudden cheerfulness about him that was almost incongruous. Having thought of him only as a sort of melancholy hallucination living on a dingy stairway, it was quite startling to see him with his face lit up like a lyric poet's, a glow of mundane exhilaration in his eyes. For the first time in our meetings he looked as though to speak to him would not break in upon his secret thoughts. He was the kind of chap, you know, who usually looked as though he was busy thinking. I remember what I said because it was so inane. Some people don't like to cross on the stairs. I looked up as I came to the turn in the steps, and said, "Superstitious?" He smiled and said "No, I guess not!"

"Only in the literal sense, at this moment," I said. An absurd remark, and a horrible pun which I regretted at once, for I thought I would have to explain it. Nothing more humiliating than having to explain a bad pun. But if I didn't explain it, it would seem rude. He looked puzzled, then his face lit up charmingly. "Superstitious—standing above you, eh? I never thought of the meaning before!"

I came up the last steps. "Pardon the vile pun," I said. Then I knew where I had seen him before, and recognized him. "Aren't you Morgan Edwards?" I asked. "Yes," he said.

"I thought so. I remember you in 'After Dinner'. I wrote the notice in the Observer ."

"By Jove, did you? I am glad to meet you. I think that was the nicest thing any one ever said." His gaunt and pensive face showed a quick flash of that direct and honest friendliness which is so appealing. We found that we were both living on the fourth floor. For similar reasons, undoubtedly. I'm afraid he thought, at first, that I was a dramatic critic of standing. Afterward I explained that the "After Dinner" notice had been only a fluke. I was on the Observer when the show was put on, and one of the dramatic men happened to be ill.

Wait a minute: give me a chance! I'll tell it exactly as it came to me, in snips and shreds. At first I didn't pay much attention. I had problems of my own that summer. You know what a fourth-floor hall bedroom is in hot weather. I had given up my newspaper job, and was trying to finish a novel. I couldn't work late at night, when it was cool, because if I kept my typewriter going after nine-thirty the old maid in the next room used to pound on the partition. I didn't get on very well with the work, and the money was running low. Every now and then I would meet Edwards in the hall. He looked ill and worried, and I used to think there was a touching pathos in his careful neatness. My own habits run the other way—my Palm Beach suit was a wreck, I remember—but Edwards was always immaculate. I could see—having made it my business to observe details—how cunningly he had mended his cuffs and soft collars. Poor devil! I used to see him going out about noon, with his cane and Panama hat. I dare say he scrubbed his hat with his toothbrush. Summer is a hard time for an actor who hasn't had a job all spring. Of course there are the pictures, and summer stock, but I gathered that he had been ill, and then had turned down several offers of that sort on account of something coming along that he had great hopes for. I remembered his really outstanding

116

work in "After Dinner", that satiric comedy that fell dead the winter before. Most of the critics gave it a good roasting, but knowing what I do now I expect the real trouble was poor direction. Fagan was the director, and what did he know of sophisticated comedy? As I say, I had reviewed the piece for the Observer, and had been greatly struck by Edwards's playing. Not a leading part, but exquisitely done.

But just at that time I was absorbed in my own not-too-successful affairs. For several years I had been saying to myself that I would do great stuff if I could only get away from the newspaper grind for a few months. And then, when I had saved up five hundred dollars, and buried myself there on Seventy-third Street to write, I couldn't seem to make any headway. I got half through the novel, and then saw that it was paltry stuff. It was flashy, spurious, and raw. One warm evening I was sitting at my window, smoking mournfully and watching some girls who were laughing and talking in a big apartment house that loomed over our lodgings like an ocean liner beside a tugboat. There was a tap at the door. Edwards asked if he could come in. I was surprised, and pleased. He kept very much to himself.

"Glad to see you," I said. "Sit down and have a pipe."

"I didn't want to intrude," he said. "I just wanted to ask you something. You're a literary man. Do you know anything about Arthur Sampson?"

I had to confess that I had never heard the name. No one had, at that time, you remember.

"He's written a play," Edwards said. "A perfectly lovely piece of work. I've got a part in it. By heaven, it seems too good to be true—after a summer like this: illness, the actors' strike, and all that—to get into something so fine. I've just read the whole script. I'm so keen about it, I'm eager to know who the author is. I thought perhaps you might know something about him."

"I guess he's a new man," I said. "What's the play called?"

"'Obedience.' You know, I've never had such a stroke of luck—it's as if the part had been written for me."

"Splendid," I said, and I was honestly pleased to hear of his good fortune. "Is it the lead?"

"Oh, no. Of course they want a big name for that. Brooks is the man. My part is only the foil—provides the contrast, you know—on the payroll as well as on the stage." He laughed, a little cynically.

"Who's producing it?"

"Upton."

"You don't mean to tell me Upton's got anything good?" I knew little enough about theatrical matters, but even outsiders know Upton's sort of producing, which mostly consists of musical shows where an atrocious libretto is pulled through by an opulent chorus and plenty of eccentric dancing. "A chorus that outstrips them all" was one of his favourite advertising slogans.

"That's why I was wondering about the author, Sampson. This must be his first, or he'd never have given it to Upton. Or is Upton going to turn over a new leaf?"

"The only leaves Upton is likely to turn over are figleaves," I said, brutally. Upton's previous production had been called "The Figleaf Lady".

"That's the amazing part of it," said Edwards. "This thing is really exquisite. It is beautifully written: quiet, telling, nothing irrelevant, not a false note. What will happen to it in Upton's hands, God knows. But he seems enthusiastic. He's a likable cutthroat: let's hope for the best. You're busy—forgive me for breaking in."

Well, of course some of you have seen "Obedience" since that time, and you know that what Edwards told me was true. The play was lovely; not even Upton could kill it altogether. It was Sampson's first. Have any of you read it in printed form? It reads as well as it plays. And the part that Edwards was cast for—Dunbar—is, to any competent spectator, the centre of the action. You remember the lead: the cold, hard, successful hypocrite; and then Dunbar, the blundering, kindly simpleton whose forlorn attempts to create happiness for all about him only succeed in bringing disaster to the one he loves best. It's a great picture of a fine mind and heart, a life of rich, generous possibilities, frittered and wasted and worn out by the needless petty obstinacies of destiny. And all the tragedy (this was the superb touch) because the wretched soul never had courage enough to be unkind. What was it St. Paul, or somebody, said about not being disobedient to the heavenly vision? Dunbar, in the play, was obedient enough, and his heavenly vision made his life a hell. It

118

was the old question of conflicting loyalties. How are you going to solve that?

I suppose the tragic farce is the most perfect conception of man's mind—outside the higher mathematics, I dare say. Everyone knows Sampson's touch now, but it was new then. Some of his situations came pretty close to the nerve-roots. The pitiful absurdity of people in a crisis, exquisite human idiocy where one can't smile because grotesque tragedy is so close... those were the scenes that Upton's director thought needed "working up". But I'm getting ahead of my story.

Well, now, let me see. I'd better be a little chronological. It must have been September, because I know I took Labour Day off and went to Long Beach for a swim. I had just about come to the conclusion that my novel was worthless, and that I'd better get a job of some sort. At the far end of the boardwalk, you remember, there's a quiet hotel where one gets away from the crowd, and where you see quite nice-looking people. After I'd had my swim, I thought I'd stroll up that way and have supper there. It's not a cheap place, but I had been living on lunch-counter food all summer, and I felt I owed myself a little extravagance. I was on my way along the boardwalk, enjoying the cool, strong whiff that comes off the ocean toward sunset, when I saw Edwards, on the other side of the promenade, walking with a girl. My eye caught his, and we raised our hats. I was going on, thinking that perhaps he wasn't so badly off as I had imagined, when to my surprise he ran after me. He looked very haggard and ill, and seemed embarrassed.

"Look here," he said, "it's frightfully awkward: I must have had my pocket picked somehow. I've lost my railroad tickets and everything. Could you possibly lend me enough to get back to town? I've got a lady with me, too."

I didn't need to count my money to know how much I had. It was just about five dollars, and, as you know, that doesn't go far at Long Beach. I told him how I stood. "I can give you enough for the railroad fares, and glad to," I said. "But how about supper?"

"Oh, we're not hungry," he said; "we had a big lunch." I knew this was probably bravado, but I liked him for saying it. While I was feeling in my pocket for some bills, and wondering how to pass them over to him unobtrusively, he said, "I'd like to introduce you to Miss Cunningham. We're going to be married in the autumn."

119

You may have seen Sylvia Cunningham? If so, you know how lovely she is. Not pretty but with the simple charm that beauty can't——

Well, that's trite! She'll never be a great actress, but in the rôle of Sylvia Cunningham she's perfect. I hate to call her slender—it's such an overworked word, but what other is there? Dark hair and clear, amberlucent brown eyes, and a slow, searching way of talking, as if she were really trying to put thought into speech. She, too, poor child, had had a bad summer, I guessed: there was a neat little mend in her glove. She was very friendly—I think Edwards must have told her about that Observer notice. I saw that they were both much humiliated at their mishap, and I judged that genial frankness would carry off the situation best.

"Life among the artists!" I said. "What are our assets?"

"I've got seventeen cents," said Edwards. It was a mark of fine breeding, I thought, that he did not insist upon saying how much it was that he had lost.

Miss Cunningham began to open her purse. "I have——"

"Nonsense!" I said. "What you have doesn't enter into the audit. In the vulgar phrase, your money's no good. I've got five dollars and a quarter. Now I suggest we go to Jamaica and get supper there, and then go back to town by trolley. It'll be an adventure."

Well, that was what we did, and very jolly it was. You know how it is: artists and actors and manicure girls and newspapermen are accustomed to ups and downs of pocket; and when they have a misery in the right-hand trouser they make up for it in a spirit of genial comradeship. Jamaica is an entertaining place. In a little lunchroom, which I remembered from a time when I covered a story out that way, we had excellent ham and eggs, and a good talk.

As we sat in that little white-tiled restaurant, I couldn't help watching Edwards. I don't know how to make this plain to you, but our talk, which was cheerful enough, was the least important part of the occasion. Talk tells so little, anyway: most of it's a mere stumbling in an almost foreign tongue when it comes to expressing the inward pangs and certainties that make up life. I had a feeling, as I saw those two, that I was coming closer than ever before to something urgent and fundamental in the human riddle. I thought that I had never seen a man so completely in love. When he looked at her there was a sort of—well, a sort of possession upon him, an enthusiasm, in the true sense of that strange word. I thought to myself that Keats must have looked at Fanny Brawne in just that way. And—you know what writers are—I must confess that my observation of these two began to turn into "copy" in my mind. I was wondering whether they might not give me a hint for my stalled novel.

There are some engaged couples that make it a point of honour to be a bit off-hand and jocose when any one else is with them. Just to show, I suppose, how sure they are of each other. And somehow I had expected actors, to whom the outward gestures of passion are a mere professional accomplishment, to be a little blasé or polished in such matters. But there was a perfect candour and simplicity about them that touched me keenly. Their relation seemed a lovely thing. Too lovely, and too intense perhaps, to be entirely happy, I thought, for I could see in Edwards's face that his whole life and mind were wrapped up in it. I may have been fanciful, but at that time I was seeing the human panorama not for itself but as a reflection of my own amateurish scribblings. In my novel I had been working on the theory—not an original one, of course—that the essence of tragedy is fixing one's passion too deeply on anything in life. In other words, that happiness only comes to those who do not take life too seriously. Destiny, determined not to give up its secrets, always maims or destroys those who press it too closely. As we laughed and enjoyed ourselves over our meal, I was wondering whether Edwards, with his strange air of honourable sorrow, was a proof of my doctrine.

Of course we talked about the new play. Edwards had persuaded Upton to give Miss Cunningham a place in the cast, and she was radiant about it. Her eyes were like pansies as she spoke of it. I remember one thing she said:

"Isn't it wonderful? Morgan and I are together again. You know how much it means to us, for if the show has a run we can get married this winter."

"This fall," Edwards amended.

"Morgan's part is fine," she went on, after a look at him that made even a hardened reporter feel that he had no right to be there. "It's really the big thing in the play for any one who can understand. It's just made for him."

She was thoughtful a moment, and then added: "It's too much made

121

for him, that's the only trouble. You're living with him, Mr. Roberts. Don't let him take it too hard. He thinks of nothing else."

I made some jocular remark, I forget what. Edwards was silent for a minute. Then he said: "If you knew how I've longed for a part like that—a part that I could really lose myself in."

"I shouldn't care," I said, "to lose myself in a part. Suppose I couldn't find myself again when the time came?"

He turned to me earnestly.

"You're not an actor, Roberts, so perhaps you hardly understand what it means to find a play that's real—more real than everyday life. What I mean is this: everyday life is so damned haphazard, troubled by a thousand distractions and subject to every sort of cruel chance. We just fumble along and never know what's coming next. But in a play, a good play, it's all worked out beforehand, you can see the action progressing under clear guidance. What a relief it is to be able to sink yourself in your part, to live it and breathe it and get away for awhile from this pitiless self-consciousness that tags around with us. You remember what they used to say about Booth: that it wasn't Booth playing Hamlet, but Hamlet playing Booth."

The next day, I remember, I tied up my manuscript neatly in a brown paper parcel, marked it Literary Remains of Leonard Roberts (I was childish enough to think that the alliteration would please my literary executor, if there should be such a person), put it away in my trunk, and went down to Park Row to see if there were any jobs to be had. Of course it was the usual story. I had been out of the game for six months, and Park Row seemed to have survived the blow with great courage. At the Observer office they charitably gave me some books to review. As I came uptown on the subway I was reflecting on the change a few hours had made in my condition. That morning I had been an author, a novelist if you please; and now I was not even a reporter, but that most deplorable of all Grub Street figures, a hack reviewer. It was mid-afternoon, and I hadn't had any lunch yet. In a fit of sulks I went into Browne's, sat down in a corner, and ordered a chop and some shandygaff. As I ate, I looked over the books with a peevish eye. Never mind, I said to myself, I will write such brilliant, withering, and scorching reviews that in six months the Authors' League will be offering me hush money. I was framing the opening paragraph of my first article when Johnson, whom I had known on the Observer, stopped at my table. He was one of the newspaper men who had left Park Row to go into professional publicity work. There had been a time when I sneered at such a declension.

"Hullo, Leonard," he said. "What are you doing nowadays?"

I told him, irritably, that I was writing a serial for one of the women's magazines. There is no statement that puts envious awe into a newspaper man so surely as that. But I also admitted that if he knew of a good job I might be persuaded to listen to details.

"As it happens," he said, "I do. Upton, the theatrical producer, is looking for a press agent. He tells me he's got something unusual under way, and he wants a highbrow blurb-artist. He says his regular roughneck is no good for this kind of show. Something by a new writer, rather out of Upton's ordinary line, I guess."

"Is it 'Obedience'?"

"That's it. I couldn't remember the name." As soon as I had finished my lunch I went round to Upton's office. It was high up in a building overlooking Longacre Square, where the elevators were crowded with the people of that quaint and spurious world. The men I found particularly fascinating—you know the type, so very young in figure, often so old and hard and dry in face, with their lively tweeds, starched blue or green collars, silver-gray ties, and straight-brushed, purply-black hair. It was my first introduction to the realms of theatrical producing, and I must confess that I found Mr. Upton's office very entertaining with its air of elaborate and transparent bunkum. I sat underneath a coloured enlarged photo of the Garden of Eden ballet in "The Figleaf Lady" and surveyed the small anteroom. It was all intensely unreal. Those framed photographs, on which were scrawled To Harry Upton, the Best of His Kind, or some such inscriptions, and signed by dramatists I had never heard of; the typist pounding out contracts; the architect's drawing of the projected Upton Theatre at Broadway and Fiftieth Street, showing a line of people at the box office—all this, I knew by instinct, meant nothing. The dramatists whose photographs I saw would never write a real play; the Upton Theatre, even if it should be built, would not house anything but "burlettas," and the typed contracts were not worth so much carbon paper. As for Mr. Upton himself, one couldn't help loving him: he was such a disarming, enthusiastic, shrewd, unreliable bandit. To abbreviate, he took me on as a member of his "publicity staff" (consisting of myself and a typewriter, as far as I could see) at one hundred dollars a week. His private office had three ingenious exits; going out by one of them, I

123

found myself in a little alcove with the typewriter and plenty of stationery. Rehearsals of "Obedience" had started that morning, Upton had told me; so before I went home that afternoon I had typed and sent off the following pregnant paragraph for the next day's papers:

Henry Upton's first dramatic production of the season, "Obedience," by Arthur Sampson, began making elbow room for itself at rehearsals yesterday. Keith Brooks will play the leading rôle, supported by Lillian Llewellyn, Sylvia Cunningham, Morgan Edwards, and other distinguished players.

I had a feeling of cheerfulness that evening. The cursed novel was no longer on my mind, there would be a hundred dollars due me the next week, and I was about to satisfy my long-standing curiosity to know something about the theatre from the inside. It was one of those typical evenings of New York loveliness: a rich, tawny, lingering light, a dry, clear air, warm enough to be pleasantly soft and yet with a sharp tingle in the breeze. I strolled about that bright jolly neighbourhood round the hideous Verdi statue, bought a volume of Pinero's plays at one of those combination book, cigar, and toy shops, and as I sat in my favourite Milwaukee Lunch I believe (if I must be frank) that some idea of writing a play was flitting through my mind. I got back to my room about ten o'clock. I had just sat down to read Pinero when Edwards tapped at the door. My mouth was open to tell him my surprising news when I saw that he was unpleasantly agitated. First he insisted on returning my loan, although I begged him to believe that there need be no hurry about it.

"Rehearsals began to-day," he said. He sat down on the bed and looked very sombre. "The worst possible has happened," he said. "Fagan's directing."

I tried to console him. Perhaps I felt that if Upton had shown such good sense in his choice of a press representative his judgment in directors couldn't be altogether wrong.

"Oh, well," I said, "if the play's as good as you say, he can't hurt it much. Upton believes in it, he won't let Fagan chop it about, will he? And he's got a good cast—they won't need much direction: they know how to handle that kind of thing."

"It's plain you don't know the game," he said. "If Upton had combed Broadway from Herald Square to Reisenweber's, he couldn't have

124

found a man so superbly equipped to kill the piece. As for poor Sampson, God help him. Fagan is a typical Broadway hanger-on, with plenty of debased cunning of his own; not a fool at all; but the last man for this kind of show, which needs imagination, atmosphere, delicate tone and tempo. But that's not all of it. Fagan hates me personally. He'll get me out of the company if he possibly can. He can do it, of course: he has Upton's ear."

He sat a moment, one eyebrow twitching nervously. Suddenly he cried out, in a quivering, passionate voice which horrified and frightened me: "I've got to play Dunbar! It's my only chance. Everything depends upon it."

Such an outcry, in a man usually so trained a master of himself, was pitiful. I was truly shocked, and yet I was almost on the verge of nervous laughter, I remember, when the idiotic old spinster in the next room pounded lustily on the wall. I suppose she thought we were revelling. I could see that he needed to talk. I tried to soothe him with some commonplace words and a cigarette.

"No," he said, "I know what I'm talking about. Fagan hates me. No need to go into details. He directed 'After Dinner,' you know—and massacred it. We had a row then... he tried to bully a girl in the company... I threatened to thrash him. He hasn't forgotten, of course. He passed the word round then that I ruined the show. If this were any other play I'd have walked out as soon as I saw him. But this piece is different. I—I've set my heart on it. My God, I'm just meant for that part——"

In the hope of calming him, I asked what had happened at the first rehearsal.

"Oh, the usual thing. We went through the first act, with the sides. I knew my lines perfectly, the only one who did (I ought to, I've been over them incessantly these few weeks—the thing haunts me). That seemed to annoy Fagan. Sampson was there—a quiet little man with a bright, thoughtful eye. For his benefit, evidently, Fagan got off his old tosh about Victor Hugo and the preface to 'Hernani'. It's a bit of patter he picked up somewhere, and uses to impress people with. In the middle of it, he suddenly realized that I had heard it all before. That made him mad. So he cut it short, and reasserted himself by saying that the first act would have to be cut a great deal. Sampson looked pretty groggy, but said nothing. Sampson, I can see, is my only hope. Fagan will try to force me out of the show by hounding me until I lose my temper and quit. He began by telling me how to cross the stage. A man who learned the business under Frank Benson doesn't need to be taught how to walk!"

I ventured some mild sedative opinion, because I saw it did him good to pour out his perplexity.

"You don't know," he said, "how the actor is at the mercy of the director. The director is appointed by the manager and is responsible only to him. If the director takes a dislike to one of the cast, he can tell the manager he 'can't work with him', and get him fired that way; or he can make the man's position impossible by ridicule and perpetual criticism at rehearsals. He remarked to-day that I was miscast. The fool! I've never had such a part."

Well, we talked until after midnight, and only stopped then because I was afraid that the spinster might begin to hammer again. In the end I got him fairly well pacified. He was delighted when I told him that I was going to be press agent, and I pleased him by making some memoranda of his previous career, which I thought I could work up into a Sunday story. To tell the truth, I did not, then, take all his distress at its face value. I knew he had had a difficult summer, and was in a nervous, high-strung state. I thought that his trouble was partly what we call "actors' disease," or (to put it more humanely) oversensitized selfconsciousness. I promised to get round to the rehearsal the next day.

As a matter of fact, it was several days before I was able to attend a rehearsal. For the next morning Upton asked me to go to Atlantic City, where he had a musical show opening, to collect data for publicity. His regular press man was ill, and it was evident that he expected me to do plenty of work for my hundred a week. However, it was a new and amusing job, and I was keen to absorb as much local colour as possible. I went to Atlantic City on the train with the "Jazz You Like It" company, took notes of all their life histories, went in swimming with the Blandishing Blondes quartette that afternoon, had them photographed on the sand, took care to see that they were arrested in their one-piece suits, bailed them out, and by dinner-time had collected enough material to fill the trashiest Sunday paper. In the evening the show opened, and I saw what seemed to me the most appallingly vulgar and brutally silly spectacle that had ever disgraced a stage. I wondered how a company of quite intelligent and amusing people could ever have been drilled into such laborious and glittering stupidity. The gallery fell for the Blondes, but the rest of the house suffered for the most part in silence, and I expected to see Upton crushed to earth. When

126

I met him in the lobby afterward I was wondering how to condole with him. To my surprise he was radiant. "Well, I guess we've got a knockout," he said. "This'll sell to the roof on Broadway." He was right, too. Well, this is out of the story. I simply wanted to explain that I was away from New York for several days.

When I got back to Upton's office I was busy most of the day sending out stuff to the papers. Then I asked the imperial young lady who was alternately typing letters and attending to the little telephone switchboard, where "Obedience" was rehearsing. At the Stratford, she replied. Wondering how many of Mr. Upton's amusing and discreditable problems were bestowed under her magnificent rippling coiffure (she was really a stunning creature), I went round to that theatre. The middle door was open and I slipped in. The house was dark, on the tall, naked stage the rehearsal was proceeding. It was my first experience of this sort of thing, and I found it extremely interesting. The stage was set out with chairs to indicate exits and essentials of furniture; at the back hung a huge canvas sea-scene, used in some revue that had opened at the Stratford the night before. The electricians were tinkering with their illuminating effects, great blazes and shafts of light criss-crossed about the place as the rehearsal went on, much to the annoyance of the actors. Little electric stars winked in the painted sky portion of the blue back-drop, and men in overalls walked about gazing at their tasks.

I sat down quietly in the gloom, about halfway down the middle aisle. Two or three other people, whose identity I could not conjecture, sat singly down toward the front. In the orchestra row, in shirtsleeves, with his feet on the brass rail and a cigar in his mouth, sat a person who, I saw, must be the renowned Fagan. Downstage were Brooks, Edwards, and a charming creature in summery costume who was obviously the original of the multitudinous photographs of Lillian Llewellyn. The rest of the company were sitting about at the back, off the scene. Edwards, who was very pale in the violent downpour of a huge bulb hanging from a wire just overhead, was speaking as I took my seat.

"Wait a minute, folks—wait a minute!" cried Fagan, sharply. "Now! You've got your situation planted, let's nail it to the cross. Mr. Edwards!"

The actors turned, wearily, and Miss Llewellyn sat down on a chair. Brooks stood waiting with a kind of dogged endurance. At the back of the stage a workman was hammering on a piece of metal. Fagan pulled his legs off the rail and climbed halfway up the little steps leading from the orchestra pit to the proscenium.

"Mr. Edwards!" he shouted, "you're letting it drop. It's dead. Give it to Mr. Brooks so he can pick it up and do something with it. You've got to lift it into the domain of comedy! My God!" he cried, throwing his cigar stub into the orchestra well, "that whole act is terrible. Take it again from Miss Llewellyn's entrance. Mr. Edwards, try to put a little more stuff into it. This isn't amateur theatricals."

Edwards turned as though about to speak, but he clenched his fist and kept silent. Brooks, however, was less patient.

"Pardon me, Mr. Fagan," he said, in a clear, ironical tone. "But I should like to ask a question, if you will allow me. You speak, very forcibly, of lifting it into the domain of comedy. That seems a curious phrase for this scene. Is it intended to be comic? If so, I must have misconstrued the author's directions in the script."

Brooks was too well-known a performer for Fagan to bully. Brooks was "on the lights"—in other words, when the show's electric signboard went up, it would carry his name. Around his presence hung the mystic aura of five hundred dollars a week, quite enough in itself to make Fagan respectful. The director seemed a little startled by the star's caustic accent. As a matter of fact, I don't suppose he had ever read the script as a whole. I remembered that after the first rehearsal Edwards told me that Fagan had admitted not having read the play. He said he preferred to "pick up the dialogue as they went along". This reference to the author must have seemed to him unaccountably eccentric. I daresay he had forgotten that there was such a person.

He threw up his hands in mock surrender. "All right, all right, if that's the way you take it, I've got nothing to say. Play it your own way, folks. Mr. Edwards, you're killing Mr. Brooks's scene there. Give him time to come down and get his effect."

Again I saw Edwards lift his head as though about to retort, but Brooks whispered something to him. Fagan came back to his seat in the front row and lit a fresh cigar. "Take it from Miss Llewellyn's first entrance," he shouted.

Miss Cunningham and a third man came forward and the five regrouped themselves. The rehearsal resumed. I watched with a curious tingle of excitement. The dialogue meant little to me, plunging in at the middle of the act, but I could not miss the passionate quality of Edwards's playing. Even Brooks, a polished but very cold actor, caught the warmth. Their speeches had the rich vibrance of anger. I was really startled at the power and velocity of the performance, considering that they had only rehearsed a week. As I watched, someone leaned over my shoulder from behind and whispered: "What do you think of Dunbar?"

My eyes had grown accustomed to the gloom. I turned and saw a little man with a thin face and lifted eyebrows which gave him a quaint expression of perpetual surprise. I was so absorbed in the scene that at first I hardly understood.

"Dunbar—? Oh, Edwards?" I whispered. "I think he's corking—fine."

At that moment Edwards was in the middle of a speech. Miss Cunningham had just said something. Edwards, going toward her, had put his hand on her shoulder and was replying in a tone of peculiar tenderness. Fagan's loud voice broke in.

"Dunbar! Mr. Edwards! I can't let you do it like that. You make me hold up this scene every time. Now get it right. This is a bit of comedy, not sob stuff. Try to be a bit facetious, if you can. You're not making love to the girl—not yet!"

There was a moment of silence. Those on the stage stood still, oddly like children halted in the middle of a game. I don't suppose Fagan's words were deliberately intended as a personal insult, but seemed to himself a legitimate comment on the action of the piece. I think his offences came more often from boorish obtuseness than calculated malice. But the brutal interruption, coming after a long and difficult afternoon, strained the players' nerves to snapping. Brooks sat down with an air of calculated nonchalance and took out a cigarette. Then a tinkling hammering began again somewhere up in the flies. Edwards was flushed.

"For God's sake stop that infernal racket up there," he cried. Then, coming down to the unlit gutter of footlights, he said quietly:

"Mr. Fagan, I've studied this part rather more carefully than you have. If the author is in the house, I'd like to appeal to him as to whether my conception is correct."

There was such a quiver of passion in his voice that even Fagan seemed taken aback.

"What's got into you folks to-day?" he growled. "Oh, very well. Is Mr. Sampson here?"

The little man behind me got up and walked down the aisle in an embarrassed way.

"Mr. Author," said Fagan, "have you been watching the rehearsal?"

Sampson murmured something.

"Is Mr. Edwards doing the part as you want it done?"

"Mr. Edwards is perfectly right," said Sampson.

"Thank you, sir," said Edwards from the stage. "Fagan, when you are ready to conduct rehearsals like a gentleman, I will be here." He turned and walked off the stage.

Brooks snapped his cigarette case to, and the sharp click seemed to bring the scene to an end. Fagan picked up his coat from the seat beside him. "Bolshevism!" he said. "All right, folks, ten o'clock to-morrow, here. Miss Cunningham, will you tell Mr. Edwards ten o'clock tomorrow?"

This last might be taken either as a surly apology, or as an added insult. Rather subtle for Fagan, I thought. As I was getting out of my seat, the director and a venomous-looking young man whom I had seen in and out of Upton's office walked up the aisle together. Sampson was just behind them. I could see that the director was either furiously angry, or else (more likely) deemed it his duty to pretend to be.

"This show's no good as long as Edwards is in it," he said, loudly, spitting out fragments of cigar-wrapper. "That fellow's breaking up the company. I sha'n't be able to handle 'em at all, pretty soon. This kind of thing puts an omen on a show."

Well, that was my introduction to "Obedience". I watched Fagan and the hanger-on of Upton's office—one of those innumerable black-haired young infidels who run errands for a man like Upton, hobnob with the ticket speculators in the enigmatic argot of the box office, and seem to look out upon the world from behind a little grill of brass railings. They moved up the velvet slope of the passage, arguing hoarsely. Sampson faded gently away into the darkness and disappeared through the thick blue curtains of the foyer. An idea struck me, and I ran behind to see the stage manager, Cervaux, who was playing one of the minor parts. I cajoled his own copy of the script away from him, promising to return it to the office the next morning. I wanted to read the play entire. Going out toward the stage door, behind a big flat of scenery I came upon Miss Cunningham. She was sitting in a rolling chair, one of those things you see on the boardwalk at Atlantic City. There was a whole fleet of them drawn up in the wings, they were used in that idiotic revue playing at the Stratford. It added to the curiously unreal atmosphere of the occasion to see her crouching there, crying, alone in the half light, among those absurd vehicles of joy.

I intended to pass as though I hadn't seen her, but she called out to me. If Upton could have seen her then, her honey-brown eyes glazed with tears, black rings in her poor little pale face, he would have raised her salary—or else fired her, I don't know which.

"Mr. Roberts," she said, slowly and tremulously—"I don't know who else to ask. Will you try to help Morgan?"

"Why of course," I said. "Anything I can do——"

"You were at the rehearsal? Then you saw how Fagan treats him. It's been like that every day. The brute! It's abominable! You know how we had set our hearts on playing this together, Morgan and I.... Now I've almost come to pray that Morgan will throw it up. That's what Fagan wants, of course, but I don't care. All I want is his happiness. I said something to him about giving up the part, but he... Mr. Roberts, I'm worried. I've never seen Morgan so strange before. He's not himself. I don't know what's the matter, I have a feeling that something——-"

The electricians were still fooling about with their spotlights, and a great arrow of brilliance sliced across the stage and groped about us. It blazed brutally upon her tear-stained face, and then see-sawed among the little flock of rolling chairs. It was that shaft of light that dispelled, once for all, the feeling I had had that this was all some sort of theatrical gibberish, pantomime stuff intended to impress the greenhorn press agent. For when she recoiled under the blow of that sudden stroke of brightness I could read unquestionable trouble on her face. There was not only perplexity, there was fear.

She was silent, turning her face away. Then she stepped down from the chair, in a blind sort of way.

"I begged him to give it up," she said, quietly. "He said that no one

131

but the author could take him out of this part. I wish the author would.—Oh, I don't know what to wish! Morgan's making himself ill fighting against Fagan."

We walked across Fortieth Street together, and I escorted her as far as a Fifth Avenue bus. As we waited for the bus she said:

"You'll probably see him to-night. Tell him about rehearsal to-morrow, ten o'clock. He had gone before I could speak to him. You see, he's not himself. We were to have taken supper together."

She added something that I have never forgotten:

"The worst tragedy in the world is when lovely things get in the hands of people who don't understand them. If you see Mr. Sampson, you might tell him that. Some day he may write another play."

When I got up to Seventy-third Street I tapped at Edwards's door. He was at his table, writing. I had intended to ask him to take dinner with me, thinking that perhaps I could help him, but his manner showed plainly that he wanted to be alone. If I had been an old friend of his, perhaps I could have done something; but I did not feel I knew him well enough to force myself upon his mood.

"Fagan sent you word, rehearsal to-morrow at ten," I said. "It sounds to me like an apology."

He looked at me steadily.

"You were there to-day? You will understand a little, then."

"I understand that Fagan is a ruffian."

"Fagan—Oh, I don't mean Fagan." He paused and looked at the wet point of his pen. "I was just writing a note to Sampson," he said. He hesitated a moment, and then tore the written sheet across several times and dropped it in the basket.

"Oh, hell," he said. "I can't appeal to Sampson again. I'll have to work it out myself.—Don't imagine I take Fagan too seriously. Fagan is only an accident. A tragic accident. That's part of my weird, as the Scotch say. I mean, you'll understand better about Dunbar."

I didn't quite understand, and said nothing.

132

"I wouldn't let a man like Fagan stand between me and Dunbar," he said. "It's in the hands of the author now. You heard what he said. He put Dunbar into the play, he's the only one who can take him out of it."

The next morning Upton broke the news to me that I was to go out as advance man. The opening was set for Providence, only ten days later. There was to be a two-weeks' tour of three-night engagements, and I had to arrange for the publicity, poster-printing, accommodations for the company, and so on. This did not appeal to me very strongly, but I scrambled together a lot of photographs, interviewed the cast as to their preferences in hotel rooms, and set off. I got back a week later. We were then only three days away from the opening. They were rehearsing with the sets, Upton's telephone blonde told me, and I hurried round to the Stratford to see how the scenic artist had done the job.

They had just knocked off for lunch when I got there, and at the stage door I met Edwards coming out with Miss Cunningham. He looked very white and tired.

"Hullo," I said; "just in time to have lunch with me! Come on, we'll go to Maxim's. I've still got some of Upton's expense money."

"I've got to rush round to the modiste for a fitting," said Miss Cunningham. "The gowns are just finished. You take Morgan and give him a good talking-to. He needs it." I did not quite understand the appeal in her eyes, but I saw that she wanted me to talk with Edwards alone. She went toward Bryant Park, and we turned down to Thirty-eighth. Edwards stood a moment at the corner looking after her.

"Sylvia says I'm a fool," he said, wearily. "I don't know: most of us are, one way or another.—You know I told you that I put my confidence in the author."

"Quite right," I said. "I myself heard Sampson say he thought you were corking."

"Well, I wonder if he's double-crossing me?" said Edwards, slowly, as though to himself.

"In what way?"

"Yesterday, when I was coming down to rehearsal, there was a tie-

133

up of some kind on the subway. The train stood still for a long time, and then the lights went out. We stayed in the dark for I don't know how long—everybody got nervous. It was pitch black, and awfully hot and stuffy. The women began to scream. I felt pretty queer myself—you know I haven't been well—and as we sat there I went off into a kind of doze or something. Then, just as everybody was on the edge of a panic, the lights came on and we went ahead. When we got to Times Square I think I must have been a bit off colour, for the damned rehearsal went out of my head entirely. Suddenly I realized I was in a drugstore drinking some headache fizz when I was over an hour late at the theatre. My God! I hustled down there as fast as I could go. Queer thing. I went in through the stage door, and as I came round behind the set I heard voices on the stage. They were rehearsing, of course. Naturally, they couldn't wait all morning for me. But this is what I'm getting at. You know that scene in the second act where I say to Brooks: It's all very well for you to say that. Ah, hah! I see! But suppose you had been in my place—-

"You know that's a turning point in the act. There's a particular inflection I give that speech—the way I say the 'Ah, hah! I see!' that makes the point clear to the audience and gets it over. Well, they were rehearsing that scene, and from behind the canvas I heard that speech. And what I heard was my own voice."

"What on earth do you mean?" I said.

He hesitated. He was sitting, his lunch almost untasted, with one elbow on the table and his forehead leaning on his hand. Under his long, sinewy fingers I could see his brows tightened and frowning downward upon his plate.

"Exactly what I say. It was my own voice. Or, if you prefer, Dunbar's voice. I heard that speech uttered, tone for tone, as I had been saying it. It was the precise accent and pitch of ironical comment which I had thought appropriate for Dunbar at that point in the action. The sudden change of tone, the pause, the placing of the emphasis—the words were just as if they had come out of my own mouth. I stopped, instinctively. I said to myself, has Fagan got someone else to play the part, and been coaching him on the side? Someone who's been sitting in at rehearsals and has picked up my conception of Dunbar? And at that moment I heard Fagan sing out 'All right, folks, the carpenter wants to work on this set. We'll quit until after lunch.'

134

"I tell you, I was staggered. If I was out, I was out, but they might have been straight with me. It was a matter for the Equity, I thought. I didn't want to chin it over with the others just then, and I heard them coming off, so I slipped through the door that opens into the passage behind the stage box. I meant to tell Fagan what I thought about it. There was Sampson sitting in one of the boxes. He saw me, and got up. He said: 'By Jove, Mr. Edwards, you were fine this morning. I've never seen you do it so well. It was bully, all through. Keep it like that, and you're the hit of the play.'

"I thought at first he was making fun of me. I was about to make some sarcastic retort, when he put out his hand in the friendliest way, and said:

"'I want to thank you for what you're doing for that part, and I know it hasn't been easy. I've never seen anything so beautifully done, and just want to tell you that if the play is a success it will be largely due to you.'

"This, on the heels of the other, astounded me so that I didn't know what to say. I made some automatic reply, and he left. I sat down in the cool darkness of the box to rest, for I was feeling very seedy. My head went round and round—touch of the sun, I dare say, or that foul air in the crowded subway car. I was still there when they came back, an hour later, for the afternoon rehearsal. I tried to talk to Sylvia about it, but all she would say was that I ought to go to a doctor."

"I think she's right," I said. "Look here, have you had any sleep lately?"

"You seem to have forgotten Dunbar's line," he said. "'There'll be 'plenty of time to sleep by and bye.'"

"For God's sake forget about Dunbar," I said. "Man, dear, you're on the tip of a nervous breakdown. Now listen. This is Friday. Dress rehearsal to-morrow. Sunday you'll have all day off. Take Miss Cunningham and go away into the country somewhere and rest. Put the damned play out of your mind and give her a good time. You both need it."

I didn't see him again until Monday morning.

I went up to Providence on the train with the company. As I passed through one of the Pullmans looking for a seat in a smoking

135

compartment, I found Miss Cunningham and Edwards sitting in adjoining chairs. To my delight, they seemed very cheerful, and smiled up at me charmingly.

"Took your advice yesterday," he said. "We went down to Long Beach again. Had a lovely day, not even a pickpocket to spoil it."

"What an unfortunate remark!" said Sylvia, laughing. "He means, not a pickpocket to bring us a friend in need and give us a jolly evening in Jamaica."

"I spoke the speech trippingly," he admitted.

"And we left Dunbar behind!" said Sylvia. She flashed me a grateful little look that showed she knew I had tried to help.

"Have you decided where to spend the honeymoon?" I asked, greatly pleased to see them so happy.

"Hush!" she said. "We'll wait till we see what sort of notices the show gets."

"Think of the poor press agent. I've used up all my dope. Get spliced while we're in Providence and it'll give me a nice little story. You know the kind of thing—'Critics' Praise Brings Pair to Altar; Press Clippings Cupid's Aid'."

"You're getting as vulgar as a regular press agent," she said, merrily. "They don't think of anything except in terms of good stories for the paper."

"Oh," I said, "the press agent has his tragedies, too. Think how many stories he knows that he can't tell."

I felt that this remark was not very happily inspired, and went on through the car calling myself a clumsy idiot. In the smoking compartment, as luck would have it, were both Upton and Fagan, smoking huge cigars and talking together. I sat down and lit my pipe. Fagan, in his usual way, was trying to impress Upton with his own sagacity. There was another musical horror of Upton's scheduled to begin rehearsal shortly, and probably Fagan was hoping to land the job as director.

"What did you think of Edwards at the dress rehearsal?" said Fagan.

Upton grunted. He had a way of retaining his ideas until others had committed themselves.

136

"I've been telling you right along, he's impossible," said Fagan. "No one can work with him. He's too damned upstage. Now I got Billy Mitford to promise he'd run up and see the opening. Billy is the man you need for that part. I had him in at the dress, and he'll be there tonight. I've given him a line on the part, and if Edwards falls down we can start rehearsing Billy right away. He could get set in a week, and open with the show in New York."

"Four hundred a week," was Upton's comment, seemingly addressed to the end of his cigar.

"All right, he's worth it. He's got a following. This guy Edwards is dear at any price. He'll kill the show. He doesn't get his stuff over. God knows I've worked on him. And he crabs Brooks's work more'n half the time. What you want is one of these birds that gets the women climbing over the orchestra rail. Billy is your one best bet, take it from me."

"Well, we'll open her up and see what we got," said Upton. "Is Sampson along?"

"No. Scared. Said he was too nervous to come. He'll learn to write a play afterwhile. What a mess that script was until I got her straightened out."

When we got to Providence I had several jobs to do around town. I visited the newspaper offices, stopped in at the theatre where the stage crew were busy unloading scenery, and when I returned to the hotel I lay down in my room and had a good nap, I was awakened late in the afternoon—about five o'clock, because I looked at my watch—by a knocking at the door. I got up and opened. It was Edwards. To my dismay, his cheerfulness had vanished. He had gone back to the old pallid and anxious mood.

"Nervous, old man?" I said. When I had booked the rooms for the company I had arranged that he and I should be next door to each other, so that I could keep an eye on him.

"Nervous?" he said. "I'm ill. Had another of those damned swimming spells in my head. Haven't got any brandy, have you?"

I hadn't, but offered to go in search of some. He wouldn't let me.

"Don't go," he said. "Look here, I saw Mit-ford in the lobby just now. What the devil is he doing here?"

137

"Perhaps there's some other show on," I suggested, miserably.

"I told you they were trying to double-cross me," he said. "I know perfectly well what he's here for. Fagan is trying to razz me into a breakdown. Then he'll put Mitford in as Dunbar. But I tell you, I'll play this thing in spite of hell and high water."

He paced feverishly up and down, and I tried to ease his mind.

"By God, they sha'n't!" he cried. "I'll put this thing up to the author. Where's Sampson?"

"He's not here. For heaven's sake, man, don't get in a state. Everything's all right."

"Everything's all right!" he repeated, bitterly. "Yes, everything's lovely. Let's 'lift it into the domain of comedy'. But if you see Fagan, tell him to keep away from me."

I begged him to rest until dinner-time. I went into his room with him, made him lie down on the bed, rang for a bottle of ice water, and left him there. Then I went downstairs and wrote a couple of letters. I was just leaving the hotel when I met Fagan coming in. He stopped me to ask if I had taken care to put his name on the playbill as director. I had. If the show was a flop, I at least wanted his name attached as a participial cause.

I wandered uneasily about the busy streets until theatre time. I couldn't have been more nervous if I had been going on the boards myself. I spent part of the time prowling about trying to see how much "Obedience" paper I could find on the billboards and in shop windows. I stopped in at a lunchroom and had some supper. The place reminded me of the little café in Jamaica where Sylvia and Edwards and I had eaten together.

My mind was full of the picture of the two, and his face as he leaned across the table toward her. I thought that I had never seen a couple who so deserved happiness, or who had fought harder to earn it. What was the subtle appeal in this play that made it react so strangely upon him? The tragedy of Dunbar in the piece, the sacrifice of the poor, well-meaning fellow whose virtue always seemed to turn and rend him, did this echo some secret experience in his own life? I wondered whether an actor's career was really the gay business I had conceived it. It occurred to me that perhaps the actor's profession is doomed to suffering, because it takes the most

138

dangerous explosives in life and plays with them. Love, ambition, jealousy, hatred, those are the things actors deal with. You can't play with those without one of them going off every now and then. They go off with a bang, and somebody gets hurt.

I suppose I'm sentimental. I wanted those two to win out. It seemed to me that a defeat for their fine and honourable passion would be a defeat for Love everywhere, and for all who believe in the worthy aspirations of the heart. I don't suppose any press agent ever pondered more generous philosophies than I did that night, over my lunch-counter supper.

Time went so fast that it was after eight when I got to the theatre. I went in and took a seat in the last row. The house, to my surprise, was crowded. I could see Upton's big bald head, well down in front, beside a massively carved lady, all bust and beads, whom I supposed to be Mrs. Upton. The élite of Providence were out in force, for Brooks's name is always a drawing card. Some of them, I feared, were going to be disappointed. It is all very well to introduce a new Barrie or a new Pinero to the playgoing public, but you've got to remember that it is bound to be grievous for those who prefer the other sort of thing.

The curtain, of course, was late, and I gave a sigh of relief when I saw it go up. Edwards, waiting carefully for the hush, had the house with him in three speeches. I have never seen better work, before or since. It was noticeable that at his first exit he got a bigger hand than Brooks at his carefully prepared entrance. The only thing that seemed to me out of the way was his extreme pallor. The silly ass, I said to myself, he hasn't made himself up properly. Then it struck me that it was probably a sound touch of realism, for certainly Dunbar would not be described as a full-blooded creature. I had read the play carefully, and had seen it in rehearsal; but I had never known how much there was in it. Strangely enough, Edwards was the only one who showed no trace of nervousness. All the others, even Brooks, seemed unaccountably at a loss now and then, trampled on their lines, and smothered their points. At first the house was inclined to applaud, but as the action tightened, they hushed into the perfect and passionate silence that is the playwright's dream. There were six curtains at the end of the first act. I could tell by the tilt of old Upton's pink pate that he was in fine spirits. I looked about for Fagan in the lobby, as I was keen to see how he was taking it, but missed him in the arguing and shifting crowd.

139

By the time the third act was under way it was plain that we had a sure-fire success. Novice as I was, I could read the signs when I saw Upton scribbling telegrams at the box-office window in the second intermission, and observed the face of Mr. Mitford. The usual slips that always happen on first nights were there, of course. In the third act, when Edwards had to take Sylvia in his arms, she seemed to trip and almost fell; and I noticed that Brooks crossed the stage and helped her off, which was not in the script; but these things were not marked by most of the audience. Dunbar, you remember, makes his final exit several minutes before the end of the third act. When he went off there was a little stir among the audience—far more eloquent than applause would have been. That beautiful delineation of a blundering high-minded failure had made its appeal.

After Edwards's last exit I felt my way out, quietly, and went round through the street and up the alley to the stage door. I wanted to be the first to congratulate him on his splendid triumph. I did not want to break in too soon, so I waited near the door until I heard the crash of hands that followed the curtain. The canvas rose and fell repeatedly as the players took their calls, while the house shook with applause. From where I stood, by the switches and buttons on the control board, I could see them lined up in the orange glare of the gutter, bowing and smiling. There were cries of "Dunbar! Dunbar!" and a rumbling of feet in the gallery. It is the only time I have ever seen an audience crowd down the aisles and stand by the orchestra rail, applauding. Then I saw why they lingered. Edwards had not taken his call.

The curtain fell again, and Cervaux, the stage manager, came running off, the perspiration streaming down over his grease-paint.

"Christ!" he cried. "Where's that fool Edwards?"

As soon as the curtain finally shut off the house I could see the actors turn to each other as though in dismay. Miss Cunningham came off, and I ran to shake her hand. To my amazement she looked at me blankly, with a dreadful face, and sat down on a trunk.

Brooks strode across the stage. "Where's Edwards?" he shouted, angrily. "Tell him to take this call with me, the house is crazy."

"Where's the author?" said someone. "They want the author, too."

Several hurried upstairs to the men's dressing rooms, and I followed. The door of number 3, on which Edwards's name was

140

scrawled in chalk, stood open. Cervaux stood stupidly on the sill. The room was empty.

"He's gone," said Cervaux. "What do you know about that?"

We could still hear the tumult of the house.

"Take the curtain, Mr. Brooks," said Cervaux. "Tell them he's ill."

I looked round number 3 dressing room.

There was a taxi standing outside the stage door. I don't know how it happened to be there, or who had ordered it, but I shouted to the driver and jumped in. I have a faint impression that just as the engine started Sylvia appeared at the door, with a cloak thrown over her stage gown, and cried something, but I am not sure.

When I got to the hotel, the door of the room next to mine was locked, but the house detective got it open without any noise. There were two men in the room. In the far corner lay Fagan, unconscious, with a broken jaw, one arm hideously twisted under him, and a shattered water bottle beside his bloody head. Sprawled against the bed, kneeling, with his arms flung out across the counterpane, was Edwards.—The doctor said it was heart disease. He had been dead since six o'clock.

THE END

www.ingramcontent.com/pod-product-compliance
Lightning Source LLC
Chambersburg PA
CBHW011513170626
46810CB00009B/3347